Song For A
Summer Night

I0598524

Mark Dennis

Also By Mark Dennis

Antihero

.

Acknowledgements

I thank my wife, Camille Dennis, for tolerating my neglect during the time it took to extract this story from the æther, as well as for allowing me such free access to the uisge baugh (ish-ka baha) all the while. To Nick: this began as our little project. Thanks to Bob Wiar for the encouragement and reading of my earliest drafts. Thanks most of all to my friend and fellow author, Jess Mowry, for the cover design, advice, criticism, and for believing in this book when it was nearly forgotten.

I freely admit my indebtedness to the writings and ideas of innumerable others for inspiration, most notable in this story being those of Soren Kierkegaard, Sun Tzu, Friedrich Nietzsche and James Joyce, all of whom I quoted or paraphrased liberally with the hope and understanding that certain people would recognize and appreciate their application. I believe this to be a legitimate literary device, not to be confused with the unfortunate and oft scandalous process of "internalization." One might find shades of many others, as well, since I'm smart, but not that smart. Mine is a hero with but one of a thousand faces. Indeed, I feel I've been little more than the vehicle for some higher power working through me. I put fingers to keyboard and one day found a story had written itself... and I ask myself still, as Kurt Vonnegut says he did, "How'd I do that?" I really have no idea. The distillation of thoughts is a time-consuming and mysterious process. Question is: Is it healthy?

Finally, thank you mom and dad for making it possible that I should ever come to a place in life whereby I might even be capable of writing a book. You've earned a paragraph all to yourselves.

*This book is dedicated to Nicholas, who
understands it the way few ever will*

Song For A
Summer Night

Chapter One

In The Meadow After Dark

"**I** know you won't let me down."

Icarus Whistler was the prodigal son of sensible birds.

"...Will you?"

Icarus Whistler was a fool. Boog Barrow spoke to him with the oily, resonating voice of a radio announcer, all full of bass and control. He smiled, his threat implicit, holding the tip of a pearly claw against the blue feathers dressing Icarus's over-inflated chest. There was a glint in the moonlight and Icarus found himself silently counting teeth. Boog turned his claw with a flick of his wrist, directing its point beneath the bird's chin, so sharp that breathless Icarus never felt it pierce his skin, ever so slightly.

"That's right, Boog, give 'em a little prick!"

Algernon Fess urged him on, giddy with violent expectations. Thin and unkempt, Algernon Fess was a long-haired black-and-white, full of nasty habits, whose tangled fur was the sort human hands were loath to stroke.

"H-hey, fellas, there's no need for the rough stuff," said Icarus, rolling his eyes downward and wincing as Boog pressed with his claw and a widening, sinister grin.

"What's a nice kid like you doing out so late, anyway?" Boog asked. "You really ought to be in bed." His look softened to one of mock concern. "You don't look so good." He retracted his claw and patted Icarus roughly on the head, then released him. Icarus's head wobbled as he breathed again.

Boog turned and sauntered away, hips swaying as each foot found its place in front of the other. He was a shaggy gold tabby, a lion in miniature, full of a lion's murderous ability. Algernon stood up to follow, raking a single claw slowly across his own throat for Icarus to see. Icarus rubbed his neck with a trembling wing, sighing relief and watching as the cats melted into the shadows surrounding the moonlit meadow. The wind blew. Tall grass hissed as it waved back and forth. There was a rumble of thunder in the distance. Icarus looked down.

There was blood on his wing tip.

Chapter Two

Ulysses

"**N**o, not like that," Peter said.

Peter Phye was bored. Standing in his room amid his many toys, Peter watched as a rabbit stared dumbly at him from a shelf. "Sit like this," he said. "And watch."

Peter propped his rabbit again and stepped back slowly.

His room was cluttered with toys everywhere, so many in fact that he barely found room for himself. There were cars and trucks, and interlocking building blocks, and spacemen and army men, and books and clothing. Worse yet, there were even old drinking cups with residue dried inside them, some spawning life in the form of furry black mold.

And the bed was messy, too.

The rabbit's head fell forward, followed by the rest of his dingy white fluff, and he toppled to the floor. Peter picked him up and flung him at the mirror on his dresser, the button of the stuffed-rabbit's nose striking the glass with a brittle *click*.

And with all he had, Peter had nothing better to do.

He knelt at his window to look out, elbows propped upon the painted wood sill. He put his face against the screen and blew through his nose.

"I'm bored," he said with a nasal sigh.

Sighs, his father had told him, for good or bad, are punctuation marks in the story of life, and that life is a story which any child -- including, and, yes assuredly, even a child like Peter Phye -- should be able to enjoy with relative ease, what with its prose structured in simple, declarative sentences. One need only find the way to enjoy it. But surely, Peter thought, that didn't mean a *child's* life should be boring all the time; and yet it seemed that lately too many a sentence was punctuated at that very sill in the very way he had just done.

It might take time for Peter to grasp the full measure of his father's metaphor.

Birds twittered outside. The sill was dirty from the weight of his elbows over the course of many sighs, as well as from the occasional rainfall that found its way inside. August was thunderstorm season in Michigan. Peter rested his chin in his hands and watched the shadows darkening the shade of green on the leaves outside, some of which twisted in an easy breeze. The day had been hot, the air still warm as it blew in gently on him through the window. Peter breathed in deeply. It carried the smell of fresh mown grass.

Not much of a yard out there, really more a woodland, with green things growing all around. A forest with a pond began within twenty of Peter's twelve-year-old paces of an old cement porch that eased the transition off the back of the house. The porch was worn on the edges where traffic was heaviest, and Peter often passed time working to dislodge stones with sticks that always proved too soft for the job. Mrs. Barrow, the lady who lived across the meadow, had marbles imbedded in the cement alongside her driveway. They were ordinary marbles, like the kind Peter already had so many of, but their being locked in stone made Peter want hers very badly. It was a generous idea, of sorts, with her never having any children of her own to be amused by them. She let Peter gouge at hers with sticks from time to time, though he had hinted once toward the use of a screwdriver or chisel or some such implement, and to which was met with a straightforward "no."

Peter stepped back from the window and looked into the mirror on his dresser. The rabbit was there. He tossed it to the floor. Peter Phye was there, in the mirror, an ordinary boy, youngish looking even for his youngish age, with dark hair to crown his head like a bowl. He pushed it back, away from his eyes, and smiled a toothy smile, like his rabbit might. ...Though it wouldn't likely be smiling now, even if it could. Peter picked him up and brushed at him remorsefully, then set him on the bed. He looked again at the mirror. The Peter there had a round face and thick cheeks, and he puffed his chest and tried to look serious, to see himself as anything but what he was so used to seeing.

How very ordinary, he thought. He let the air out with a slow, deflating hiss. He always saw himself as a child and couldn't seem to change that.

Light was growing faint inside. Evening was quietly bundling color. Peter turned again to the window. Amber and orange shone through the trees, pyre for another dying day, and no cares for the morning; it was summer vacation.

What to do? thought Peter, and that was truly among his only concerns for some time now.

Cheet-cheet-cheet-cheet.

A cricket began chirping from somewhere nearby.

"I hear you," Peter said, and turned to find him.

Cheet-cheet-cheet-cheet.

Peter dropped to his hands and knees.

Cheet—Cheet—Cheet.

A little louder now. There were plenty of places to hide. Peter groped about in the waning daylight, and soon the entire woodland was alive with song, its many different melodies pouring in through the open window: buzzes and hums, music Peter had noticed before but never really heard. More than music, it was a symphony, held together by an undertone of chirps, and a solitary bullfrog, which went, gonk, gonk, gonk.

There was a rustle. A bird landed in the bush outside. Peter was too busy moving toys to notice. He felt around in near darkness under his dresser, finding both familiar and unfamiliar things. He hadn't been bothering to look at all the things he felt, which was actually a bad way to conduct a search.

Cheet-cheet-cheet-cheet.

He figured he'd know a cricket when he felt one.

The bird in the bush outside watched for a second or two, then let out with a quirky, quick song of its own...

"Po-tweedle-leedle-leet!"

It was loud, being so close, and surprised Peter, who bumped his head on a drawer that was sticking out and felt something odd *snap* between his fingers. There was the flutter of wings. Peter rub-bed his head.

And then...

There was silence.

Chapter Three
The Cat's Dissonant Nocturne

There was something different in the air that night: the rustle of leaves as a summer breeze blew. Peter lay awake and listened. The wind broke in waves, splashing through the trees and in through his window, washing over him; a silence, only relative, of subtle sounds, noticeable only on the most quiet of nights.

As was this night.

The refrigerator hummed in the kitchen, while the clock tip-toed away with the hours... Tick... Tick... Tick... Peter listened as his heart beat: Bump... Bump... Bump... marching in step with the cadence of Time.

The refrigerator stopped with a shudder and there was the rustle of leaves outside. Tick... Tick... Tick... Tick... And the ticking of the clock.

It was all so disconcerting, a silence so devoid of life and living that Peter couldn't even find sleep within it. He had to organize his thoughts. They ran hither and thither, like the children in his classroom when the teacher was late coming back from lunch. Roland Plessinger was one of those children, wild and unruly, and always on the teacher's bad side, running afoul of every rule and confinement.

Peter listened to himself breathing... The bellows of his lungs pulling... Then pushing the air, loud now in the relative silence. He heard his father's breathing from clear across the house... he sounded like he was being strangled. Peter listened and couldn't help but think.

"Meoww... woww... woww!"

Peter jumped. His father's snoring stopped with a snort. Peter's heart paused for a second, and then took off again.

What was that? he thought, his mind all awhirl: a sound utterly paralyzing in its dissonance, and just outside his window! His heart alone raced on, its frantic beating making him feel warm in the stomach, and in his face and neck. He lifted his head... But there was only silence and a ringing in his ears. He waited... And the ticking of the clock and the renewed hum of the refrigerator... The sound of the breeze blowing outside, stirring the leaves in sibilant gusts.

Peter listened... Silence... Nothing more.

His father began again to snore deeply. Peter lay his head back and closed his eyes. His cantering heart eventually slowed to rejoin the ticking clock... and wasn't that just like a skittish little chicken heart, always ready to fly at the least sign of danger! Peter was actually working to control that, which was a challenge, especially at night, since he'd heard the silly stories about a Devil Dog and ghosts that roamed the woods of the Deepest Forest, trans-migrated (it was widely supposed) from their shadowy epicenter in the haunted ruins of the old cement factory in Marlborough, amid which certain kids at school claimed to have camped and seen and heard the spooks first-hand. His father told him the stories were all nonsense, just pap for the wide eyes and gaping mouths of babies, which was all logical and satisfactory enough during the daytime in familiar surroundings. Sure, it was clear... then... that the oaf who had fed it to him was the only thing to be worried about, and that anecdotal accounts didn't amount to real scientific knowledge, and that scientific knowledge was the solid basis of a real world... talk which, by the way, served only to confuse and enrage the oaf: "We *are* talkin' about science," he'd said, "you dork! What're *you* talkin' about!? Ever hear a' the paranormal?"

But at night, while the whole wide world slept instead of you...

Well, one could never know for sure. Peter just wished he hadn't heard the stupid stories in the first place. So he thought of pleasant things instead: there were red and green kites, and ice cream cones, and wind blowing in his ears. Peter was Superman...

"*Meow... woww... woww... woww!*"

Peter's eyes snapped open. ...A cat! he decided in that instant. He heard footsteps from his parents' room.

Boom! Boom! Boom!

His father's snoring had stopped again and he was rumbling through the house, causing the things in the curio cabinet to clatter, and making no effort to quiet his passing. Peter heard him muttering as he thumped through the kitchen, and then the *bang!* and the *scooch!* of a chair, followed by the angry sibilants of stifled cursing. A light flicked on, suddenly revealing the things out back through his window, the old tree and the wood pile, and a few things Peter had never noticed before.

There was the squeak of the back door. Peter heard his father grunt. ...And then, a second later... the clang of a tin can hitting the wood pile.

"Ray-*Owww*!"

And the shriek of a cat.

"And *stay* away!" his father yelled.

Peter slipped out of bed and knelt to watch through his window. Bushes rustled at the back of the yard. The screen door banged shut. Things went black again. Peter hurried back into bed and pulled the sheet to his chin, then listened as his father passed. ...And then, to the brief, indiscernible murmurs coming from his parents' room. Their bed squeaked twice. The murmuring stopped. Peter closed his eyes and there were...

Once more...

The sounds of silence.

Chapter Four
Harpy

Peter awakened next morning to the clatter of dishes, the subtle *boom* of cupboards closing, and the smell of something burnt in the air.

His mother was up.

Peter rolled out of bed and stood in the brilliance of morning pouring through his window. Seeing the early sunshine always made him happy. Sleep was never all that important to him, more a nuisance than anything else, always sneaking up and trying to steal him away. He reached for his shorts, crumpled on the floor, and stepped back into them for the fourth straight day now... and he was quietly proud of that. He fished through a drawer for a clean T-shirt, though. He'd gotten grease from his bike chain on yesterday's and made it too dirty – "useless," in fact, some might choose to say (as his mother had) -- useless enough to be the reason for a well-punct-uated lament at the window sill the night before. If only he hadn't tried to show up for dinner in it. His mother could be surprisingly critical of certain things... as far as Peter was concerned. He wonder-ed how she was feeling.

Better go to the kitchen before she comes to get me, he thought.

Mrs. Phye stood at the stove with her back to the room, rasping with a metal spatula on a cast-iron pan, the scent of something burnt lingering more heavily there. On the days when she was up early to cook, Peter knew to tread lightly. There was an angry brute within his mother, a thing that couldn't be rational. It held her and kept her distant from others. It made her frightening and unpredictable, and Peter, who loved her because she was his mother and he a little boy, always wished it was different.

He looked around. Mrs. Phye was a messy cook. The curtains were drawn and the lights were on, adding to a profoundly depressive atmosphere. There was an ever-present mountain of things heaped in the sink and on the counter tops, and the smell of something not quite right, most noticeable when one came in from the outside. The family usually washed what it needed as they were ready to use it, or used it dirty (in Peter's case) if it didn't look *too* dirty. The implication of running water was a thing that might stir his mother's ire.

"Is that my breakfast?" Peter asked.

His mother turned with a start, her frizzy hair bound with a red bandana, a signal, Peter knew, to beware. The floral pattern of her short blue nightgown was faded and shabby, and her thin, shapeless legs looked long as they emerged from beneath it. She was barefoot, with long toes and untidy nails. Peter looked at her feet and thought of how he hated the sight of feet.

"Peter!" She pointed her spatula at him. "I've told you not to sneak up on me like that! You know I'm not feeling well!"

Something brown fell to the floor from her spatula. They both glanced down, and then quickly up again, into one another's eyes. Mrs. Phye's eyes narrowed as her chest heaved and she wheezed against the sudden rush of excitement. "Now sit down and behave yourself!"

Peter's mother suffered frequent and diverse maladies. So many that it was pointless to ask about them except to be polite. Peter sat. His mother put a plate down in front of him, along with a last irritable look and a half glass of milk.

Burnt toast, Peter thought. And eggs! Oh, and what an awful

mess it was, sitting there, charred and reeking of smoke. The tastes, the textures! Peter could feel his throat constricting in anticipation of it all. He looked from his plate to his glass. Even that wasn't right.

"Mom, can I have..."

"Get up," she said with her back to him, "and get it yourself."

Saying no sure came easy to some, and Peter noted his mother had dozens of ways of saying it, none of which sounded very polite. Not that being denied could ever sound polite to his thinking, and he gave her that much. But when he wondered why that was, why she said no to everything, it seemed clear to him that it was because it was easiest, and that a person had to consider more than the immediate ramifications when saying yes, a process which might in itself become fatiguing. "No" held the status quo better and rarely upset future plans for things like naps and television shows. "No" fell easily from the mouth. "Yes" had to be ejected. "No" was the least labor-intensive of all possible answers.

Peter got up and walked to the pantry, where he found the chocolate powder, then to the counter to find a spoon. He slipped one carefully out from under a stack of plates and wiped it on his shirt before using it to stir chocolate into his milk. He slurped it as he sat again at the table and grimaced when his lip caught something hard stuck to the bottom. He set it beside his glass and a puddle of brown pooled on the table beneath it.

"Well, well!" boomed a cheery voice. "And what will it be today?" Peter's father emerged from the hallway and tapped his hand with a folded newspaper he held. He was a thin, pot-bellied man, with an ordered air about him, and who always smelled like soap. He lifted Peter's spoon by the dry end and held it between his thumb and forefinger, away from his body with a pained expression, then turned and set it into the sink with a clatter.

Peter ate with his head down. "Nothing," he replied, more quietly than his father.

"Nothing? Well, I'm sure you'll find something," Mr. Phye said in a dangerously jovial tone, rubbing his fork in a napkin then unfolding his paper with a smile and a crisp snap. Peter watched as he disappeared behind it, and wondered, as he saw the writing on the back, what day it was. The idle days of summer were so easily spent, and, although young, Peter was suddenly struck by that.

"How about we check out the woods today," Peter suggested.

Mrs. Phye chuckled with her back to them. Mr. Phye lowered his paper and peered over the top at Peter, then smiled and raised it again.

"I have to work," he said.

It was worth a try. Peter's father never really cared to go out-side, except to mow the small, sparse patch of yard around the perimeter of the house, that minimum token which he insisted all civilized folk maintained. He stopped frequently when he did that to wipe his forehead with a handkerchief. It was comical, really, to watch the constant strained expression on his face as he pushed the mower along, dust and junk shooting out from under it, a pained expression which didn't remove itself until hours after he was done. He sat and breathed heavily in that time, waiting for the perspiration to dry.

Peter convinced him occasionally to go exploring with him into the woods out back. Mr. Phye was smart, and taught Peter things while they were out together. He told him what the Indians used to do, and how old certain trees and rocks were, and wasn't even fazed by the occasional prehistoric clam shell Peter dug up from the ground while in search of Clovis spear points, those Cadillacs of all Indian arrowheads, elusive and as wildly coveted one of those would be. That and Pops Barnsworth's lost gold tooth, which his father assured him was a myth, and which nonetheless always helped to spur enthusiasm for archeological digs.

But they never stayed out long... at least, never long enough for Peter. His dad would get tired, or cold or hot, or had other things to do, which seemed true enough. Peter always knew his father to be busy. He was always tinkering with a hobby, or thinking, or reading and writing things down. He always said he was busiest when he seemed least busy... even, in fact, when his eyes were closed. Peter knew he meant in his head, and he liked his dad, because although limited physically, he was fun to talk to and to be around.

But now his dad was trying to remain invisible, hiding behind a newspaper.

"Dad, I heard a cricket in my room last night."

"Humph," his father replied.

Peter chewed, and read the car ads on the back of the paper. "I heard you, too," he said through a full mouth.

Mr. Phye lowered his paper to look at Peter, then raised it again. "Humph."

"I heard that cat. Whose was it, dad, Mrs. Barrow's?" Peter waited.

"Don't know," his father said slowly from behind his paper.

"What'd you throw at 'em, dad, a soup can or something?"

"Um-hm."

Peter stopped chewing and turned to look at his mother, who had stopped scraping on the pan on the stove. Peter realized his reckless lack of propriety, and of the risk it posed to his father.

"Yep," came the lazy response from behind the paper. "Soup can, I think. ...We had soup yesterday, didn't we?"

The paper crackled as he closed it to turn a page.

Mrs. Phye turned with a plate full of eggs and toast and set it down brusquely in front of him. Mr. Phye lowered his paper and folded it, his cloak of invisibility now vanished. "Thank you," he said with an unsuspecting wink and a smile as he took a big bite of scrambled eggs. ...Then cringed. He tried to hide it with a clumsy grin. Mrs. Phye glowered. Clumsy was definitely the word for it. Peter felt a twinge of guilt. Mr. Phye took a bite of toast and chewed and looked up, and nodded uncomfortably. Mrs. Phye continued to stare. "Very good," Mr. Phye said through the food he chewed. "Um-hm."

"Is there something else you want to say?" Mrs. Phye demanded.

"...What? ...No. ...Why?" Mr. Phye asked, swallowing hard.

"Yep. Soup can, I think. We had soup yesterday, didn't we?'" Mrs. Phye honked like a goose as she flung his words back at him.

"Oh... No, no, no," Mr. Phye responded quickly, a weak response really, defensive only in the sense of one ready to absorb blows. "I only meant it was the first thing I grabbed. ...The can, I mean. It was right there. It was either that or a dish, or... And... Never mind."

Then, with the faintest indication of assertion, "Peter, when you're done, could you please go outside and see if you can find the can I threw? I shouldn't have done that. It wasn't very nice. And throw it away for me, please." He gestured with a thumb over his shoulder and a sheepish grin, then lowered his head and never looked up or said another word.

Mrs. Phye flew immediately into a rage, slamming cupboards and cookware, and talking to herself about things like her life and her family and the future, all in a most distressing light. It was hard on the digestive tract, as Peter well knew, to eat under such duress. He and his father hurried through their breakfast and left the house together as fast as they could, his father saying good-bye to him on the porch, then walking stiffly to his car.

Chapter Five
The Sea Of Queen Anne's Lace

Peter milled around outside all by himself. He held a long thin stick in his hand and brushed the grass with it as he paced back and forth. He spied the soup can lying in the pickers behind the wood pile, so worked his way through them, sideways and backwards, threading a hand slowly through the barbs until he could barely grasp the can between his index and middle fingers, all the while allowing every picker in the bush to set itself along the length of his outstretched arm. And there he hung, pondering his next move, poised as he was with every subsequent movement clearly more perilous than the last. His father might be less eager to toss cans around if he had to work like this to get them back his own self, and Peter thought he might mention that to him. He worked his way back out again, the pickers grabbing his clothing and clawing his skin, seemingly with malice, no matter how hard he tried to avoid them, and the madder he got, the fiercer they fought, until...

"Darn it!"

Peter tossed the can toward the house and wiped a streak of blood from his forearm as he finally tore free. The air was muggy for such an early part of the day; the kind of air, he knew, that might promise brutality later, sticky and pressing down, heavily laden with moisture and ready to burst. His scratches mingled with sweat and began to sting, but he couldn't rub them because they oozed. He untucked his shirt and fanned himself with it, taking his time to look about. To the left was a meadow. He wandered the short way through the trees and stood at its edge, where the weeds were grown up tall. Bees buzzed busily about the wild flowers there, and things were still wet with dew. It was a large meadow, at least two football fields in every direction, its vastness broken only by the top of an ancient blue Chevrolet parked in the middle. Peter waded through the grass toward it.

He placed his palms on the bulky fender. The metal was hot and there was a dusty coating on the surface that didn't quite seem like dust. Peter rubbed, then looked at his fingertips, then wiped them on his shorts. He looked at his fingers again. They were still dirty. Peter went to the door and pulled on the handle, and the door gave with much resistance and a splintering creak. He stuck his head inside. The car smelled old, or at least he related the smell to old-ness, because the car looked like nothing he'd ever seen on the road before. It was a sunken ship, as it were, come to rest in the meadow long before he could ever remember. He climbed in and pulled the door shut, and once inside it was nearly unbearable, what with the sun pounding the car like an anvil and turning the air to steam... which is impossible to breathe. Peter rolled the window down by the stiff old crank at his side, then slid across and did the same on the other side. He grasped the wheel in both his hands, a thin, knurled, hard plastic wheel that flexed and felt like it might break if he chose to twist hard enough. He looked out over the hood, through a dirty but otherwise unblemished windshield, and the glass glowed along its top and bottom with the faint colors of a rainbow. The only other things to see were weeds grown all about... Queen Anne's lace, with their clusters of white atop green stems.

An ocean of grass and flowers, thought Peter.

His car was a ship, and Peter imagined himself captain, sailing a boundless sea of grass. Wind tossed him on the white-capped waves. He gripped the wheel, turning it fiercely, first right, then left, then hard right.

"Batten down the hatches!" he called. "We're in for a bumpy ride!"

A bug flew in and struck him on the cheek -- "Ow!" -- and in that instant Peter thought he must have known how Admiral Lord Nelson felt, getting this and that shot off while commanding his ship. Wow, quite a shock. He closed his mouth and dropped his hand from the side of his face, and looked in the mirror to see if it had left a mark. Not really. A little red, maybe. He looked down at the seat beside him and there was the culprit, a blue bug walking in circles, apparently stunned koo-koo itself.

"Holy cow!" he said. "You might've put my eye out, flying around that way like a stray bullet! Don't you watch where you're going?" And then he became Admiral Nelson again: "You're late, you know! You're lucky I don't have you keel-hauled. Now gather your wits, we have work to do." He looked forward and made the sound of a churning motor, turning the wheel and throwing his body roughly back and forth. It was fun for a time. A very short time.

"I dare say, Mr. Bug, we may very well melt!"

But the day's reality re-captured him. Peter wiped his forehead. It was hot! Time to move along. He pushed the door open, again with a groan and a splintering creak.

"Bye, Mr. Bug," he said. "I wish you were really my first mate, and we were really on an adventure. But it's hot and I gotta go." Peter pushed the door shut. "I'll leave you in charge now." He saluted. "Carry on."

Peter waded through the Queen Anne's lace, toward the place where shade might offer respite.

Chapter Six

Polyphemus

"**W**ho said you could sit in my car, Phye?"

Peter hesitated without turning to look. He didn't need to. He stepped as quickly through the weeds as fast as he could without appearing to run.

"*Stop*, Phye!"

Peter stopped and turned slowly around. He held his hand up to shield his eyes from the sun and panned the trees along the far side of the meadow from whence the voice had come.

"Oh, hi, Pixie," Peter called. "Your car? No I wasn't."

Peter used as composed a tone as he was able, and yet his heart had picked up considerable speed beneath his sticky shirt. He wondered how he'd managed to get caught so unawares. Pixie Anderson was about as stealthy as a bulldozer, his comings and goings normally heralded by loud talking, heavy footsteps and cracking twigs. And yet here he was, lurking somewhere in the shadows. This was no way to start a day! thought Peter, and these were just a few of his more discernible thoughts, since his mind was, in fact, reeling with blurred thoughts and fragmented suggestions, all superimposed, one on the other and jumbled up – spurred by a cantering heart

— some crazy and some more practical, things like, *No. No! Friendship. Offer to play with him? No way! Run? Not yet. Run! No. Wait. Calm...*

"Hey. ...Ah, Pixie. ...Where's Rex?"

Pixie Anderson wasn't much of a playmate for a normal child. He was the sort of boy other children hid from, a grunting Neanderthal who caused mothers to snatch their kids inside when they saw him coming; the sort of boy whose first inclination toward conflict resolution was a rap on the skull; the sort of boy who confuses the paranormal for real science... who scoffs at the scientific method and embraces Devil Dogs right in broad daylight!

"Never mind, Phye, I saw you," said Pixie, emerging into the daylight, heavyset and tall for his age, which was a full year more than Peter's. He held an apple in his hand, a big, green, wild apple from one of the trees along the edge of the meadow. "You gonna lie to me now?"

Pixie tossed the apple up and down as he walked.

"Hey! Betcha don't know where t' find a rainbow today?" offered Peter.

"Who cares!"

Of course *he* wouldn't! thought Peter, searching even more desperately for some small token, for any idea, knowing full well that silence played against him and that Pixie was likely to fill it in any way he saw fit.

"It's not your car!" Peter blurted, shocked by his own audacity. He hadn't recalled confrontation being among his many reeling thoughts and suggestions. And, as he stood there, blaming his mouth for the betrayal, Pixie caught the apple and just stared, more shocked than anyone. Peter stepped back, his sensibility returning, slowly at first, melding now to a single, familiar, practical thought.

"What, Phye? You callin' me a liar?"

Peter turned and ran. Pixie fired the apple he held -- its apparent purpose all along -- striking Peter squarely between the shoulder blades. The blow broke poor Peter's stride and he bowed his back, just like the soldiers in old movies when they were shot, then fell face-first to the ground. And there he lay, beneath the Queen Anne's lace, writhing and gasping in a vacuum. He rolled over and in his agony saw Pixie standing above him, silhouetted against the brilliance of sunshine, his round, smirking face set against a bright blue sky. Peter tried to speak, but only gaped, the anxiety of breathlessness deepening a primal fear within him. He opened his mouth like a fish out of water, red-faced and bulgy-eyed, and nothing but spent air continued to escape for a full ten or twenty seconds, and in that time he was certain he would never breathe again.

He heard the ruthless grunts that passed for Pixie's laughter, while Pixie placed a toe against his forehead and forced his face sideways into the ground. Peter smelled the earthy scent of meadow grass.

"Aw, little crybaby gonna tell his daddy?" Pixie everted his lower lip in an infuriating pouting expression, then pushed harder with his foot. And then Peter snapped. He caught a breath (and something else he hadn't realized was in him), and thrashed and scrambled, and in a hazy exchange found himself wrapped around Pixie's legs, driving him to the ground, Pixie shuffling backward, arms flailing like a useless pair of propellers, before falling hard. The two grappled -- only briefly -- more a frenzied attempt on Peter's behalf to escape before clambering to his feet and launching himself onward off Pixie's stomach with a squishy "OOF!"

"You die, Phye!" came the strangled threat.

Peter waded, unabashedly and as fast as he could, through the sea of Queen Anne's lace while Pixie hurled vile epithets.

Chapter Seven
Birds On A Wire

There they all were, Icarus Whistler and the others, loafing on the wire above the barber shop on the same languid day Peter had the wind knocked out of him by Pixie Anderson. They just sat and stared, the birds, a flock of ne're-do-wells, dividing their time between dozing and doing nothing, noticing and wise-cracking at every little thing that went on below. Squeak was one of them.

"Hey Icarus," he said, "looky there."

Icarus opened an eye and looked across the street. A fat pigeon sat alone on the wire there, looking very dull and aloof.

"Oaf," remarked Icarus, then closed his eye again.

Squeak inhaled deeply and flexed his wings as he arched his back. "Nearly got two branches off the ground today, Icarus," he said as he exhaled, looking proudly from one to the other of his wings.

"*Twigs*, Squeak," someone said. "Twigs. Stop exaggerating."

Icarus just smiled with his eyes closed. "That all?" he said.

Squeak blinked with a puzzled expression. He was small and thin for his age, and had a prominent overbite. The discrepancy between his upper and lower jaws caused him to drool a little as he stared with his mouth open. Squeak was always trying to build himself up by lifting fallen twigs into the air and bragging about it to Icarus.

"I figured you for, like, six or seven by now. Look at you," Icarus said with a smirk. "Lemme see your wing."

The other birds chuckled.

Squeak looked around, hesitated, then raised a wing and pushed his feathers back to reveal the puny white flesh underneath.

"*Whoa!* Guys, look at the muscles ripple!" Icarus said.

Squeak looked at his wing and smiled, while the others jabbed one another, working hard to maintain their encouraging expressions.

"Hey Squeak, I know, see that guy down there?"

Squeak squinted with his mouth open as he looked down. Icarus winked at the others. "Go on down and see if you can lift the hat off his head."

"Yeah Squeak!" someone shouted, "Go on, do it!"

"Yeah! Yeah! Yeah!"

And all the birds began a noisy clamor.

Squeak lowered his wing and fluffed the feathers back, eyes steadily fixed on an old man walking along the sidewalk below. He had just come from the barber shop, and was adjusting a baseball cap onto his head. He wore denim coveralls, and shuffled slowly with bowed legs apart like his feet hurt. Squeak pursed his beak and darted from the wire like an arrow.

Icarus and the others broke into expectant snickering.

Squeak dived down and snatched feebly at the old man's hat, but couldn't lift it. The old man reacted and smacked Squeak with a sweep of his hand, causing him to crash to the sidewalk in a fluttering heap. The old man gave him a kick as he flopped about, and sent Squeak skidding into the street, where a car swerved with a *toot* and barely missed him... all of which was followed by a rumble on the wire.

"Ho-ho-ho! HO-HO-HO! Was that funny or what!?" cried Icarus, slapping his side. Squeak righted himself and shook his unsteady head, then flew onto the gutter of the building across the street.

"Whoa, whoa," said Icarus, "here he comes, guys. Hold it down."

Squeak flew back, and everyone on the wire was grave looks and seriousness. Squeak studied them all carefully, not knowing what to say... being careful, in fact, not to say too much, because he was still a little goofy and not exactly sure what had happened, or, more importantly, how it had *looked*. "Man, was that a lucky shot or what?"

His punch-drunkenness did little for his compromised dignity. The others stared for a second, then broke into hysterics.

"That old boy clobbered you!" roared Icarus. "What the heck did you..."

"Hey, Icarus!" a voice called from below.

Icarus looked down and stopped laughing. "Whatta *you* want?"

"Mom says y' gotta come home. Y' didn't finish cleanin' up like you were supposed to."

Icarus's kid brother, Stevie, called up to him from a wire below. Stevie, in addition to being a model child, was a mole. Not literally, of course, but in the colloquial sense. Stevie, in his capacity as his mother's eyes and ears, and by his own count, was at least partly responsible for one-hundred-and-sixteen punitive cuffs to his recalcitrant brother's ear. They had a very conscientious mother.

"Go on, get outta here y' little brown-nose!" yelled Icarus.

That made the score one-hundred-sixteen to zero by conservative counts, and hence, the degree of enmity.

"Mom said!" was Stevie's wearisome reply.

"Get *outta* here!" Icarus dived down and knocked Stevie off the wire. Stevie fluttered downward, then recovered with carefully controlled form and a perfect wing-spread, making haste all the while toward the sanctuary of the family's nest.

"You're in trouble!" he cried as he flew away. "I'm tellin'!"

"I'm *tel*-lin'" mocked Icarus in a whiney voice, and chased after him in large, swooping circles, while the others burst forth to follow in a noisy, freeform cloud.

Chapter Eight

Transformation Chamber

Mrs. Phye watched out the back window as Peter made his way through the trees. He wandered slowly, talking to himself, tapping the trees with a stick as he passed, stopping to turn things over on the ground every now and then, and squatting to have a look underneath.

She looked at the clock on the kitchen wall: two o'clock.

She thought she loved her routine. And yet, she knew it was killing her. She looked about the house, then turned and went quickly down the basement steps.

Chapter Nine

The Enchantment

Peter lay awake in the pale darkness of his bedroom. He watched as the moon shone brightly and the wind blew fast-moving clouds along a hurried course. His window was open and a cooling breeze blew from outside, sustaining his curtains gently inward. Lightning flashed in the distance. Thunderstorm weather.

Peter noticed the silence between subtle rumbles, the same as the night before. There were no other sounds, except those of the wind and the hiss of the leaves. And the rumble of approaching thunder. No chirping, no croaking, no buzzing.

Fireflies glowed.

Peter turned and watched them in his dresser mirror, against the wall away from the window, fireflies, drifting quietly. First here, then there, then there.

Like his thoughts.

Peter opened his eyes and couldn't remember closing them. The pale green lights, no longer here and there, were merged now into a single large light that bobbed like a cork in the center of his silvery mirror.

That's weird, he thought, and dreamy thoughts slowly gave way to lucid ones. He opened his eyes wide and sat up. The green glowing light emerged from the mirror and stopped, floating in front of him, no bigger than a golf ball.

"You're not a firefly," Peter said.

A little man hovered, smiling in the glow of his own light.

"Are you a fairy?" Peter asked.

"In essence," replied the man in a tiny, musical voice.

Peter just stared.

"I've come to give you your wish, Peter, to give you something to do," the fairy said.

Peter blinked. He couldn't recall a wish. "H-how do you know my name," he asked in a whisper.

"Everyone knows who Peter Phye is," the fairy answered. Then he smiled. "Look at yourself in the mirror."

Peter pushed his sheet aside and stood at the dresser. He had never seen himself in the dark before... or couldn't remember noticing at least. He looked different that way, less like the Peter Phye he knew than some stranger.

"Look real hard, Peter. Pretend you don't know the one you see there. See yourself as another might."

Peter stared hard at himself (it took some doing to do it just right), and soon he was mesmerized. He stared, and the more he stared the more separate he became from the one in the mirror. He saw himself for the first time with impartial clarity. Peter was a thought without a body; the image of himself, but *another*, watching, taking on a life of its own, until, in time...

"Hello, Peter," his reflection said to him.

Peter turned to look at the fairy, who was not reflected in the mirror, and who waved toward it with a smile. "Don't be afraid," he said. "It's you."

Peter looked again at his reflection, which held out its hand. Peter held his own hand out and they touched at the glass. Peter blinked. His reflection blinked. The fairy smiled brilliantly, still hovering in his soft green glow, then flew away through the window into the nighttime breeze.

And Peter never remembered closing his eyes.

Chapter Ten
Dreamland

Peter dreamed he was outside, sitting in a bathtub, washing himself in moonbeams, bathing in the aura of another place and wondering how to dress himself when he was done.

Wonder what's for dessert tonight? he thought.

A breeze blew softly from the north. Peter turned to face it, feeling ticklish as the air gently tossed his hair. It was cool but not at all uncomfortable. He closed his eyes and spread his arms and thought he was flying. He felt it in his stomach and in his mind, and Peter was, for all intents and purposes, flying.

"Welcome," a voice said.

Peter opened his eyes. A kind-looking woman stood before him, smiling. She wore flowing white robes and had golden iridescent hair. Peter was with her, suddenly in a happy place, filled with sunshine and laughter. There were ships with sails on an ocean, and airplanes with propellers pulling colorful pennants, buzzing slowly across a warm, blue sky. There was a lopsided sun that wore a jolly grin, with all the flowers reaching for him, petals stretched outward.

"Where am I," he asked.

"You're in my home," said the woman.

"I'm Peter Phye," Peter said, "and I think I know you."

"You do," she said. "And I know you."

Peter looked around. Tiny little people with wings, no bigger than gnats or flies, swarmed about, telling him of all the wondrous things to do. Peter brushed gently to scatter them. He saw round, brightly-colored fish swimming through the air with thick lips pursed and fins waving. And beach-balls rolling on the ground, filled with laughter that escaped through faces red with the effort to contain themselves. Cheerful elves, wearing pointy hats and bushy white beards, hurried to fill them again and again and again. There were stilt-walkers with legs so long they reminded Peter of his shadow at dinner time. People were running and playing, most of whom wore bed clothes, and leaping into the air, held aloft by magic in their flights of fancy.

"This is a dream," said Peter.

"It is," the woman said.

"Are you an angel?" asked Peter.

"I am the Queen Of The Night," she said. "We visit in your dreams."

Peter thought about that for a second. "My dreams are your dreams? ...*Hey!*" he said, "That's my mom!" He pointed to his mother, running in circles with her arms spread wide, laughing. He had never seen her that way before.

"Sure it is," the Queen said. "She's here every night, and sometimes during the day, too. ...She comes in through the back door," the Queen added in a whisper, then put a finger to her lips.

"May I?" Peter asked, looking at his mother over the Queen's shoulder. The Queen smiled and extended her arm. Peter walked over to his mother.

"Oh, Peter, how wonderful you're here!" she cried in a voice almost totally unfamiliar to him.

"What are you doing, mom?"

"Nothing, really. And everything I ever wanted to!" she said, then ran around Peter and laughed like a child.

"Can I play, too?" he asked, excited to see her so.

"Yes! Take my hand!"

29

And together they leapt into the air, tumbling round and round above the ground. Peter laughed with his mother for awhile, the feelings of weightlessness tickling his stomach, until he had another idea. "Mom, I want to ask the Queen another question," he said.

"Sure, honey, I'll be right over there," his mother said, then did somersaults in the air, her feet never touching the ground.

Peter bounded with a single stride to where the Queen was watching. She clapped her hands and smiled as he approached.

"I think I like this place better than my home," Peter said.

"It's only a place to visit, though," the Queen replied.

"But I think I'd like to stay," he said.

"You can visit any time you like, but you can't stay. My walls are too thin. There's not substance enough here to nurture a boy forever. In here I only wash away the cares of one day to make you ready for the next." The Queen looked down.

"What's wrong?" Peter asked.

"Winter's coming," she said. "I feel it from the north."

"But it's still summer," said Peter with a sudden sense of urgency, the mere mention of winter evoking thoughts of dark, cold days -- and even colder nights -- with nothing but the wind to listen to. He thought of the trees, all made into something frightening, with their long, gnarled fingers rasping hideously against one another in the night. And of the shadows they cast that crept about his yard and into his bedroom. ...Cold showers and cold floors on bare feet... Darkness devouring foreshortened days.

"The music, Peter, it's gone away..."

The Queen's voice was fading.

"I can't hear you," Peter said. He reached, but he was falling. The Queen faded from view, her voice sounding like a crying child. Peter was falling, the tiny wings in his stomach all aflutter.

Peter landed into wakefulness, stirred by the dissonance of a cat outside his window.

Chapter Eleven

Amoeba

The day began hazy, with a cloud-like mist settled over the meadow. Peter's father had waked him early, chasing the cats away again. Then later, by shutting his window before the rain came. The noisy yawling, which Peter had woven as best he could into the fabric of his dream, was hideous, though cats seemed to think it pleasing. Peter woke to them, and to his father yelling, "Git! Git! Go on, *Git!*" in a loud whisper. He was gone to work now, and Mrs. Phye hadn't yet left her bed.

Peter stood in the back yard, looking toward the meadow. The moon still shone in the western day-lit sky, and was almost as big as the rising sun, which glowed orange and was burning off the mist and cover of clouds. It had rained hard the night before, with all the drums and cymbal crashes dreams could incorporate. The ground was still wet, and there were twigs and small branches with green leaves strewn about, telltale evidence of a very blustery night. But Peter had slept through all that and couldn't recall a thing.

As he stood, he looked in one direction and saw the moon and what was left of the night. And when he turned, he was able to see what a new day promised as the sun blazed away, still just a docile giant at an early hour. And he found that when he stood just right, he could see both at the same time, and chose to walk in the direction leading between them, away from the meadow filled with its treasures and perils.

A wheelbarrow was there ahead of him in the weeds. Peter tiptoed through and lifted it by both handles to turn it on its side. It was heavy and he gave a quick jerk, causing water – *standing water -- to slosh out and soak his shoes and socks and bare legs. He dropped the handles in a panic and shuffled backward, due entirely to a certain opinion he'd formed a little while back regarding standing, stagnant water. He'd looked into a microscope at camp last year and seen every manner of nasty little thing wiggling and jiggling and whipping and propellering along in drops of puddle water, drops collected from an ordinary puddle just outside the science lab window, hairy paramecium and those disgusting mosquito larvae by the score. There was nothing filthier than standing water, and Peter knew it. Just about anything might be reconstituted by it and stirred from primeval dormancy, or just come floating by and land in it. At least that was what Peter took from the lesson, which in itself might have made it valuable, because the point of the lesson was otherwise rather vague, amounting to little more than a game of hide-and-seek to the rest of the class, full of "*Ooobs!*" and "*Check it outs!*" and scurryings back-and-forth to each other's microscopes, as well as an exasperating preponderance of false amoeba sightings, each of which causing an exponential rise in the amoeba's stock. In fact, thanks to all the fervor, Peter accidentally drove the high-power lens of his microscope through the glass slide he was looking at in his haste to sort through the shapes and be the first to deliver a bona fide, phagocytizing, amoeba. It seems squishing the glass coverslip against the slide with water in between causes an amoeboid effect when seen through a lens. Until it breaks, of course. Needless to say, Peter got a harsh look from the teacher and criticism in place of kudos that day.

He kicked and brushed at the water on his legs, then studied the ground under the wheelbarrow, which was a perfect square of dry dirt. Nothing grew there, and in the place of weeds three toads huddled together. Peter reached down and picked one up, and held it close to his face. He stroked the back of its bumpy head with a finger, saying softly, "Hello, Mr. Toad. Didn't mean to scare you."

Mr. Toad didn't seem scared.

"Betcha we'd be better friends than anyone else I know around here," Peter said. He had thought before of keeping the toads as pets, but couldn't think of a better place to keep them than under the wheelbarrow, where he knew he could always find them. Mr. Toad's throat pulsed as he and Peter stared at one another. Peter blew air in his face. Mr. Toad peed.

"Nice!" said Peter, shaking off his hand.

He set the toad down, and struggled to twist the wheelbarrow back to place. It fell with a *whish* and a hollow *clump*. Peter sniffed his hand, and then wiped it on his shorts. He walked along, pushing the wet weeds aside with his feet as he moved toward the pond, through the trees, away from his house. He thought of how there was never any grass growing under the places where toads lived and wondered if they ate grass. He looked through the woods. The pond was there, not too far away, difficult to see though, through the trees and all the leaves. It was most visible in winter, when he and his father sometimes skated on it. He continued working his way through the trees and brush, remembering how the ground would become soggy nearest the water -- remembering how he'd gotten stuck in the mud once, with each heavy step causing him to sink deeper. He'd even given a passing thought to the possibility of being caught in quicksand; that's how bad it had been. Getting out was quite an ordeal, and cost him a cowboy boot -- a *pair* of cowboy boots, for that matter. He limped home with his one muddy boot on, going squish-flap! squish-flap! squish-flap! -- that's what his mother told his father she heard as he went by the window -- "squish-flap! squish-flap! squish-flap!" She hadn't been happy with Peter. She didn't like him getting dirty, or losing his clothing.

Peter looked down at his tennis shoes, wet already. He looked up and there was a relatively clear path leading between two gigantic oaks, their trunks thick with rough bark. There was a rustle in the weeds between them. The ground looked dry there, so Peter decided to follow the sound and go that way.

Chapter Twelve

Pixie Anderson And His Pets

"**O**h no, Mr. Toady looks hungry, Rex. I don't think he ate today. ...Or yesterday. ...Or the day before!"

Pixie Anderson laughed his grunting, snorting laugh, while his dog, Rex, panted. They were in the old corn-crib behind his house, a rickety structure with a pitched, corrugated tin roof; Pixie's playhouse now. It had held corn in the days when everybody farmed and raised livestock, before the Andersons lived there. Dr. Anderson, Pixie's father, was a physician with an office in town, where he saw people from as far away as three surrounding counties. He was understood to be a pretty good doctor, though anyone who knew Pixie the way Peter did would have doubted his ability based on his son's behavior. Dr. Anderson had more an aptitude for medicine than child rearing, though not many faulted him for that.

Inside the corn-crib, an emaciated, solitary toad squatted in the corner of an enormous, dirty fish tank, the fifty-gallon type, longer than tall, which sat on top of two blue plastic milk crates which Pixie had taken (without asking) from behind crabby Mr. Jenkins's store, the grocer in town who was never anything but stern looks and no nonsense. Sunshine stole into the shed through gaps between the warped, one-by-four slats that made the walls, and around the door. The bottom of the fish tank was lined with dry, parched earth, a few rocks and pebbles, and brittle grass and twigs. And parched earth it was indeed, for along with nothing to eat, there was not a single drop of water.

"C'mon Rex, let's get Mr. Toady some breakfast."

The toad watched as Pixie and Rex walked out and closed the door behind them.

From outside the shed there was the sound of talking as they returned a short while later:

"...and when I tell you to attack, Rex, that means go for the *throat*. There's no sense biting clothes or non-essential body parts. ...I heard about a dog, once, that bit this guy's..."

The door burst open. Pixie propped it with a big rock so he could see better inside. White dust particles swirled about, drifting in every direction, illuminated by the starkness of daylight streaming in.

"Now watch this, Rex." Pixie lifted the screen atop the tank and tossed a worm in. The worm twisted desperately against the hard dirt, but to no avail. The toad arched its back and stood on tip-toes, then lurched forward with surprising alacrity, greedily packing the worm into its mouth with its two front feet.

"Cool! Look at 'em go, Rex!"

The worm kept wiggling out from between the toads lips, and the toad shoved it back down each time, his front feet having become an equally useful pair of hands.

Rex just stared and panted.

"I make killer toads, Rex, assassins. I catch 'em and if they're tough enough t' graduate Boot Camp, I make killers of 'em. ..C'mon, let's get some more. I want an *army* of assassin toads!"

Pixie and Rex disappeared out the door again, slamming it shut behind them and flipping the latch.

"...I saw this movie, once, about these crazed worms that ate these people. They crawled out through their eyes..."

The toad sat in the coarsely filtered daylight, packing the stubborn worm back into his mouth, again and again and again.

"...That's right, Rex, you can only feed 'em enough t' keep 'em alive. Keep 'em hungry, that's what I say. They stay alert that way. And mean. I heard about these monkeys once, when this guy brought 'em a birthday cake..."

Mr. Toady stuffed the worm back into his mouth.

Chapter Thirteen

Between The Oaks

Peter emerged from between the oaks the way he had when he found his dad's soup can in the pickers... backwards. He had to fit himself through sideways with his arms tucked and duck beneath the full leafy branches of whip-saplings, which scraped and scratched his hair and cheeks on the way through. It was not the easy route he had anticipated. In fact, it wasn't even really very dry, what with all the residual wetness hiding in the leaves and falling on him. And so, Peter's head was down and eyes were closed as he emerged, blowing and sputtering, thanks to a spider's web and a careless open mouth.

Finally settled, Peter turned to look. He had never entered from that exact point before, and was surprised by what he saw. He was immediately reminded of a particular instance in his life which showed him how disorientation could result from sudden exposure to newness; *sudden newness*, he'd concluded afterward, being by degrees, really nothing more than a form of the unexpected. In that particular instance, Peter's mother had changed her hair color, from blonde to jet-black brunette, and Peter couldn't keep from staring at her. It was like watching another person act like his mom... and not doing a very good job of it. Her staring back at him that way threw his mind into a state of phantasmagoric agitation, a state somewhere between begrudging acknowledgement and outright disbelief; and what he was looking at now, on the other side of the tangle of brush between the oaks, was making him feel that exact same way: weird and dizzy. It was like nothing he'd ever imagined, and certainly like nothing he expected. It was as if he had found his way to another world, a world full of...

Animals, he thought. And he was prepared to accept that.

"Welcome to Efemera," a dignified voice said.

Peter looked down. A woodchuck sat smiling, with thick sideburns that flowed into a bushy mustache to cover his mouth. Peter was among many animals, all gathered together.

Peter's second thought -- which might just as easily have been his third had he believed he'd actually heard the woodchuck *speak* -- was that they were all very much unlike that senseless brute of Pixie's, Rex, trotting around with his private parts all exposed. That was the problem, Peter was thinking, with short-haired breeds of dog: no modesty. And that was very unpleasant to Peter... which was his opinion, right or wrong. And that was the difference with what he thought of these animals. They no longer seemed wild. Their fur coats and wings and body shapes, and colors for that matter, all appeared more suited to them as clothing.

"You're just in time," the woodchuck said, confirming to Peter that he had indeed spoken. "The Muse Laureate is about to read. Follow me." He waved his arm, then turned away on all fours, walking the way animals normally do.

"You're speaking English," Peter said.

The woodchuck stopped and looked at Peter. "*Heh-heh-heh*, of course I am," he said with a chuckle.

"But I can understand you," said Peter.

"Good," said the woodchuck. "That means we're speaking the same language." He winked at Peter, then turned again to lead the way.

Peter hurried after him. "But I don't understand *why* I understand you."

The woodchuck stopped. "Now I'm confused," he said.

"I've never understood you before," said Peter.

The woodchuck looked surprised. "What?" he asked.

Peter shook his head. "No."

"Well then, why have I been talking to you all this time?"

Peter shrugged.

"Hmm, and I thought you were listening," said the woodchuck. "Well, anyway, let's go. We don't have time to waste. The Muse Laureate is ready to read." He waved Peter on as he turned and scurried away.

"Read what?" Peter asked as he hurried to follow.

"A poem, of course."

The gathering crowd of animals was converging on a clearing near the pond, all apparently to hear the Muse Laureate read. Peter looked about as he moved carefully through them. The animals all spoke to one another, and Peter understood the things they were saying. Some looked at him and smiled. Others nodded politely.

A poem, Peter thought.

He was only vaguely familiar with poetry, limericks mostly, and nursery rhymes. And the naughty couplet Roland Plessinger had left on the chalkboard, which made the whole class laugh. ...Until the teacher walked in and noticed it. She had studied it for a few seconds with her weight on one foot, quietly tapping the toe of her other shoe, hands clasped in front of her, two forefingers poised like a church steeple, touching her lips. Then, calmly, she made a lesson of it, taking out chalk and correcting the grammar and punctuation, improving the word choice and rhyme scheme. And, by time she was done, it meant more homework for Peter and the rest of the class, who were just as quick then to condemn their little poet.

"And who's the Muse Laureate?" asked Peter.

"A fey that composes poetry," replied the woodchuck. "And I'm the Commodore," he said, stopping and turning to bow politely to Peter.

"Oh, thank you," said Peter. "And I'm Peter Phye."

"I know," said the Commodore. He turned and continued on. There were many creatures along the way, and not all of them animals. Peter noticed fairies, like the one he'd seen in his room the night before, flitting about, tiny people with wings, no more than a few inches tall, zipping above the chattering crowd. Peter slowed to watch one.

"Feys," said the Commodore, stopping to look back. "You've probably never seen one while awake before."

"I think I did last night," said Peter, reaching out a hand to one. It stopped to hover above his open palm. Peter blew gently on it, and it giggled then darted away.

"Fairies or feys?" asked Peter as he hurried to catch up.

"Same thing," answered the Commodore. "Just depends on what neck of the woods you come from." He talked to Peter over his shoulder as he zigged and zagged through the crowd. Peter had to work to keep up.

"Is this a dream?" he asked.

The Commodore laughed quietly, his body shaking as Peter watched from behind. "No, not exactly," he said.

"What then?" Peter asked.

"Dreams are really not things distinct from what you do and see while awake. You're only taught they are. This is all as real as you let it be." The Commodore stopped and smiled at Peter. "After all, what could possibly be more real than the things in your head?"

Peter hadn't really believed he was dreaming, because he kept trying to convince himself it was real, whereas one normally took a dream to be real without question -- in fact, often had to convince themselves it wasn't real – until they were awake, that is, before it evaporated. And that's exactly what usually happened. Peter found his dreams so airy that he could literally watch them evaporate faster than he was able to gather them into his real-time memory, like exhaust plumes out a car's tailpipe in winter. He figured if he could capture every nuance of his best dreams, he could easily be the next Dr. Seuss one day. But they always left him, or just remained as rambling, lackluster vestiges that even he found boring to retell. And when they were gone completely, they left a palpable void in his recollection, one that he had to step around and could reach into, but could never really grab hold of again.

"Isn't a commodore the captain of a ship?" Peter asked.

"Close," replied the Commodore. "It's actually a rank above captain."

"But how can a woodchuck in the middle of the woods be a naval officer?"

The Commodore clasped his hands behind his back and tilted his head, looking upward. "I cannot fiddle, but I can make a great state from a little city." He looked at Peter. "Themistocles," he said. "I admire the books in your father's library."

"My father's library?"

"The room with all the books," said the Commodore.

"Oh, those are my mom's books," replied Peter.

The Commodore raised a bushy eyebrow, "Really," he said, thoughtfully. "Anyway, we don't have time for that now."

With a gesture of a paw, the Commodore invited Peter to be seated on a fallen log. Peter sat, and then the Commodore, and soon the crowd was hushed as a tiny fairy appeared, hovering above a large, polished stump serving as a stage. The fairy hovered, bobbing slightly here and there like the small bees Peter watched in the morning while the mist was settling.

"The Muse," whispered the Commodore.

Everyone applauded briefly then fell silent. The Muse began:

> So sad, the annual,
> This crisp, rarefied day.
> Winter's coming
> To steal you away,
> Queen dowager of ephemeral beauty.
>
> Who to recall your splendor
> When Time's duress
> Fades the petals
> Of your pretty dress,
> Proud flower of yesterday's modernity?

The fairy hesitated uncomfortably and seemed to search for words:

Look at Mr. Dung Beetle roll the ball of filth he's found,
Quickly he rolls it, round and round.
Who would covet such a prize?
And yet he frets for lack of size.

Poor, poor Sisyphus, doesn't even pretend to exist;
His prize, like mine, a thread that binds,
Round the neck it twists:

No Kingdom Come, this stumblebum,
No barnyard in the sky.
The world needs offal movers,
And we should wonder why?

There was silence when the Muse was apparently finished. The Muse was tentative, looking like he might have more to say, then bowed suddenly and flitted away into the trees. It was, to Peter, like watching someone trot along nicely, and then suddenly start stumbling, fall, and then stand up, pull their pants down and bare their buttocks to the crowd... although he would be quick to say he was no expert at that sort of thing. The Commodore looked straight ahead with a stunned expression, as did everyone else, then rolled his eyes toward Peter without moving his head.

"That was so directly to the point!" someone cried from the crowd in a weepy voice.

"Yeah, it's about me!" cried another, and soon the entire woodland was sobbing.

"Doggerel!" exclaimed the Commodore. "Was that one poem or three? Is *this* what we've come to? Immortals afraid to live? Mortals afraid to die?"

Peter looked around him, at the sight of all Efemera reduced to tears. "I didn't get it," he said. "Who's Sisyphus?"

"Good for you," said the Commodore. "Because I got it and it was downright depressing! Ever since the music went away this is how it's been! Anxiety. Dread. Melancholy. Depression. *Bad poetry*!

It's a sickness, it is! We've never known such things! Regret for the past?! Fear of the future?! Whatever happened to the now of yesterday!"

"The music went away? What music?" Peter asked, alarmed by the Commodore's show of temper, and still not sure of how to respond appropriately.

"You haven't noticed?" asked the Commodore.

"...I'm not sure."

"The Music of the Night, of course. Goodness sake, don't tell me you haven't been kept awake all night by that cat's awful yawling."

"Oh, I have heard *that*," replied Peter. "It keeps my dad awake, too."

"And what about the silence when it's not carrying on? You *must* have noticed that?"

"...You know, now that you mention it. ...I just couldn't put my finger on it. But you're right! It's been terribly quiet."

"Worse than a winter's night. By golly, who can stand that for very long? Lousy, troubled sleep... I dream of things like numbers and safety pins, and mirrors reflecting into mirrors! I dreamt I couldn't keep from looking up while everyone else was looking down, and that I fell into a hole because of it! And I guess I should consider myself lucky to even have a *lousy* dream, since some say, instead of Dreamland, they've slipped off to Oblivion, where not so much as even a thought existed, and were pulled from it only by the birds with their singing in the morning. We'll all go insane with worry! The Maestro's gone missing and we don't know what to do! The concert season is so short already, and now... Who knows? His absence has driven us all to despair!"

"Who's the Maestro," asked Peter.

"The one who conducts the orchestra," replied the Commodore in a more composed tone. "Surely you've heard him."

Peter looked up as he thought for a second or two.

"He orchestrates the growing season, and without him, I'm afraid all will soon wither again. There are those among us who only have this one season."

Panic, again, began to take hold of the Commodore. His eyes

searched Peter's, which faltered ever so slightly. Peter was a bit frightened himself, thinking of groping in his bedroom without a single thought of music or maestros on the eve he first noticed the silence. He thought, with a shudder, of the odd *something* that had snapped between his fingers.

"I'm sure he'll be back," Peter said. It was the only thing he could think of to say.

"Oh, do you really think so?" the Commodore said. "Do you?" He knelt in front of Peter with paws clasped. "Because I don't know how much more I can... we can stand." And the Commodore began to cry with his head down.

Peter wasn't really sure he did think so, but he truly hoped he did. "Yes," he said. The Commodore's crying was making him feel uncomfortable. "I really think so."

Chapter Fourteen
Efemera

Those in attendance eventually regained themselves and somberly, silently dispersed, thinking of things they hadn't thought of before, making the crowd unified, and all but consolable.

"This is Efemera," the Commodore said to Peter, "where everyone has an opinion, though rarely their own anymore."

Peter was still a bit overwhelmed. "It seems like such a small thing to upset them so," he said.

The Commodore studied Peter's face. "Out here, in the middle of nowhere, you see, a crowd mentality is virtually unknown. I've had some experience with crowds, though. Something brings them together, and suddenly, *boom!* there you have it, a mob looking for a reason. And believe me, they can become focused on the littlest things."

"I think I know what you mean," said Peter, thinking of the kids in his classroom. "Is Efemera a city, then?"

"More a state, really. It is what it is, this place, this particular day, this particular time of year. Do you know when again it will be that everything is exactly as it is today?"

Peter thought for a second. "Dunno," he said. "A million years or more, I suppose. ...If not way more." He was thinking as big as he thought realistic. Purposely. After all, anyone could bandy big numbers about -- and they did – but what they were really throwing around were just words. He'd noticed some people rendering stupendous numbers ineffectual by wanton abuse, which seemed to him a form of irreverence, if not plain foolishness, and he didn't want to seem a fool or irreverent in front of the Commodore.

And then the Commodore announced: "Never! *Never again!*" causing Peter to raise his eyebrows in enlightened surprise.

Touché. He hadn't suspected that number. And by a little quick reckoning, it made sense. Thanks to math class, not only had he been given a feel for what an eternity might be, but math itself had led him to conclude zero to be the exact geographic midpoint of infinity, and whether positive, negative, real or rational, or irrational or imaginary, or whatever kind of number might still exist out there undiscovered, zero was the number Peter would always understand best. And zero was his favorite number for that reason. He hoped to expand its usefulness one day and be the first to find a way to do division by it.

"You've arrived at a once in a lifetime moment," the Commodore said. "And that's the only certainty I can think of in the entire Vast Expanse! Ninety-nine-point-nine percent of everything you normally see and do every day is summarily forgotten, even though it may seem important to you at the time. Each subtle nuance and all the little thoughts and feelings engendered. Did you know there was actually an infinity contained within a moment? That there are moments *within* moments? We're part of a moment for you, one of many, and I bid you, try to enjoy your time here." He clapped Peter on the knee. "Make of it what you will."

They sat together where they had been all along, on the fallen log, in front of the polished stump which had served as a stage.

"I'm sorry to say, though, that this is not our finest moment. We here seem to have found ourselves immersed in an era where more emphasis is placed on the actors than on those who create the characters. We're up to our ears in rhymesters who fall flat. ...Why they even make words up just to fit a rhyme! And all the unbearable clichés! I don't think I can stand one more 'nodding daisy' or 'sun-drenched afternoon!' Our art has become imitative and senseless!"

Peter hadn't thought much about such things before.

"Maybe it's just that it's... (Peter wondered what was wrong with rhymes?) ...too new," he suggested.

The Commodore looked at him with an eyebrow raised.

"*Avant garde*," he said. "No, our art is changed for the worse, and we suddenly see our lives for what they really are: worthless, nothing but leading to a meaningless end. And we dread it! Entrees in a food chain for some great monster of energy. Oh, how I long again for the bliss of ignorance!"

There was no consoling the Commodore. And though Peter understood little about poetry, oddly, he found the Commodore more poetic than the Muse laureate.

"Is there no way to change things back?" he asked.

The Commodore threw his hands in the air, "Sure," he said, "just find a way to stuff the genie back in the bottle!"

Peter stood up and wandered a few steps, and as he looked around it occurred to him that there was plenty he had never noticed before.

"Where are the fairies now?" he asked.

"The what? ...Oh, tending to their daytime duties."

"And they'll come home later to sleep? Where do they live?"

"No, no, they don't sleep," the Commodore said, distracted and trying to contain a somewhat impatient tone. "They have night-time duties, as well. They engage in tasks at all times, that's their pleasure. ...We used to look forward to sleeping, once upon a time, and to our dreams, the animals and I, but now..."

"Who takes care of their children while they're gone?"

"Fairies don't have children. They can't. Don't need to. Fairies don't get old, and they were never young. The number of fairies that exist now is the same as it ever was, and will ever be."

"How can anyone never have been born and never die?"

The Commodore smiled as though he had given that question some thought and was prepared to try to tackle it.

"We see our lives through very narrow eyes," he said, philosophically. "If you know what I mean. Mustn't all things have beginnings, you wonder, even if they have no end? And that is the thing, indeed." The Commodore rubbed his chin, distracted as he thought for a second. "Trapped in time," he said quietly to himself. "It's being said that we're all lineal descendants of the instant of creation, plowing headlong into some indefinable void, more infinite than the infinite itself. Some say that should make me feel special, that I should embrace it, and yet I feel more like I woke up to find myself caught in a bursting bubble, an insignificant speck within something momentarily whole, ready any minute for annihilation. And it fills me more with despair than it does joy, I'll tell you. 'But what's the whole without its parts?' they say, and 'What's the matter with dreamless sleep?' It's mind-boggling, with the only alternative being..."

The Commodore trailed off and studied Peter for a second or two.

"And what of you, Peter?" He leaned forward and whispered, "Do you ever think of... *The Forever?*"

"The Forever?"

The Commodore looked embarrassed at the sound of the words. "Never mind," he said, sitting up straight again. "Just a thought. ...Ehhem," he cleared his throat. "And I apologize for my behavior back there," he said, looking forward and above Peter with his paws clasped behind him.

"Oh, you mean after the..."

"Yes."

"That's all right," said Peter.

"No, it most certainly is not," said the Commodore, looking now at Peter. "And I'll try to contain myself from now on. But I must admit, we here are a bit scared. Uncharted territory, you know. I've never felt my mortality before. Used to be, whatever happened, happened. But now it seems everything must have a reason. And consequences. By golly, who wants to think of those all the time?"

Peter nodded. Those were great burdens and wreckers of fun. He'd been learning about consequences since the first time he got his hands slapped.

"And they look to me for answers," said the Commodore. "This crisis has shaken our community right to the palace."

"The palace?" asked Peter.

"The Queen," replied the Commodore.

"Oh, I met her in a dream."

"She tries not to let on," the Commodore continued. "But there are rumors of her closing down the growing season... you know, canceling summer... shutting us down and unleashing winter." The Commodore stopped again and looked scared. "I mean, it's one thing for you, living right on into The Forever, but what of the one-timers? This is it for them. And what about me? I mean, this could be it for me, as well. I've seen five winters already, you know, and that puts me up there. I won't even be able to close my eyes for fear of creeping Oblivion. At the very least, I'll be stir crazy by mid-winter's eve."

"What do you mean by The Forever?" interrupted Peter.

The Commodore raised his head as he thought, then smiled.

"I'm not exactly sure," he said. "Funny, I've heard it talked about, but I've never really known exactly what it was, or what it might even be. More a feeling than anything. A hope. Supposed to be a happy place." He chuckled. "Probably just more foolishness," he said, "the way they all talk now. After all, how could anyone possibly be happy forever? You wouldn't even recognize it for what it was after awhile..."

He stopped short and seemed struck by what he'd nearly finished saying, and looked urgently at Peter.

"You said the fairies live forever," said Peter. "Wouldn't it be like what they do?"

"They don't really 'live' forever, they're just a permanent part of The Everything," said the Commodore, waving his arms broadly. "Not living to them is as inconceivable as living forever is to the rest of us. Anyway, living forever, and living *in* The Forever are totally different."

"They are?"

"Oh sure."

"But how?"

The Commodore paused.

"Wow, that's another tough one," he said. "I was actually told that by a cardinal... it's easy enough to say and to listen to. ...Guess I never gave it enough thought, though. ...I mean, I can *feel* the difference, but it's hard to put into words." The Commodore paused for a long while. "I'm sorry," he finally said. "I need to defer that one to the thinkers of the churchyard. The monk parakeets have a cloister there. They like to give their opinions on these kinds of things."

Peter waited for a second or two as they stood in silence, looking out over the pond.

"I suppose being happy is only relative," he finally said. "How else could a poor person ever be happy and a rich one not?"

The Commodore looked at him and blinked.

"We've gotta find the Maestro," said Peter.

"Now there's an idea," said the Commodore. "Tell you what, there's a meeting this evening and you're invited."

Chapter Fifteen
Metamorphosis

It was nearly suppertime when Peter emerged from the woods. The color of the day and a gnawing in his stomach told him so. He had missed lunch, and as he walked and wondered what he might have for dinner, he heard his mother's voice coming from the front yard, talking loudly but not angrily. Peter walked along the packed gravel driveway, which was still wet, between the side door of the house and the garage.

"Here's a little drink for you, too! Ha-Ha-Ha-*HA!*"

Mrs. Phye trumpeted like a quacking duck as she laughed a raucous laugh, spraying her flowers with an equally blustery stream from the hose. Her face was red and she swayed unsteadily, her clothing soaked where she had gotten water on herself.

"Mom, what are you doing?" Peter asked. "You're spraying too hard. You'll knock all the petals off!"

Mrs. Phye looked at him as he rounded the corner of the house, her eyelids droopy and eyes unfocused. "...Oh! Peter. Peter, there you are. Wanna a drink, too? *He-He.*"

Mrs. Phye giggled mischievously, thick tongued, with her words stuck together in a messy heap as she pointed the hose at Peter, then stumbled backward and fell. "Oopsy," she said as she struggled to stand again. Peter hurried over to help. The hose was making her and the ground all around her wet. Peter took it from her and threw it to the side.

"Stand up, mom, what's wrong with you?" he asked as he pulled on her arm.

"Ow! *Ow*, Peter! Not so hard."

Peter stopped pulling, and she wallowed in the mire she had created for herself. Peter tried to lift her from behind by the armpits, but only slipped around in the mess, making himself as wet and dirty as she was. He stood and looked about with mingled feelings of helplessness and relief: nobody else was there to see.

Peter began again to struggle to lift her, when his father's car crunched to a stop on the gravel and Mr. Phye hustled out.

"Oh-oh, Peter, your mother's not feeling well again," he said, looking around as he stooped to lift the bawling, bellowing Mrs. Phye. "Ah, how long has she been out here? ...Ah, like this?"

"Dunno, dad. I just came from the woods and heard her."

"Don't worry, son, just open the door for me. Quickly please."

Mr. Phye limped onto the porch, holding Mrs. Phye up from behind, her coarse laughter from a few minutes earlier having become a slur of belligerent protestations, growing ever more angry.

Peter's father shuffled with her across the front porch and into the house. Peter hurried back down the steps and stood in the yard, scared out of his wits to go inside. His father appeared in the doorway again a few seconds later, leaning out and waving anxiously for him to come inside as he looked back and forth along the road. Peter hurried in, and his father closed the door quickly behind him.

Chapter Sixteen
Dillon Hopper

"I'm Dillon Hopper, The Fourteenth, from a long line of Hop-
pers residing in the banyan trees of the Deep South."

Dillon Hopper spoke with the lazy drawl of the old black men
who'd sat behind Peter at the Tiger's game his father had taken him
to. One had had a deep, gravelly voice and offered to buy Peter an
ice-cream, even though they didn't know one another, saying to Mr.
Phye, "That boy sho' looks like he could use an *ahhs*-cream. Whatta
y' say?" He was real nice, and taught Peter a thing or two about the
game of baseball that day.

"Are you a katydid?" Peter asked Dillon.

"No, a magicada."

"Oh," said Peter with a puzzled expression. Dillon Hopper
looked like the bug he'd seen the day before in the old car in the
meadow, and he'd been trying to account for him ever since.

"I play diddley-bow instead a' fiddle," said Dillon. "That's the
major difference."

"Oh," said Peter. "What's a diddley-bow?"

"Just a little one-string my granddaddy taught me t' make. My
whole brood were masters with cigar-box guitars and such. ...I was

transplanted here. *Misplaced*, as it were, by a thoughtless boy, in a plastic jug. But I don't hold that against *you*."

"...Oh." Peter was intrigued. "Will you play for me?" he asked.

Dillon smiled, opened his blue vest, but then looked around. His smile faded and he pulled his vest closed again. "Not now," he said quietly. "The others here have a poor appreciation for music."

Peter looked around. Some of the animals were watching, nudging one another with wry, sarcastic looks. It made Peter think of the time he'd tried out for the baseball team, and he understood at once the reason for Dillon's reticence. ...Peter had been one of two to be cut from the team last spring.

It was dusk, and within a clearing surrounded by trees, green leafy vines wove about the branches and enclosed the place where all were, once again, gathered. Fireflies, all alight amid the leaves above, twinkled as the evening breeze gently tossed them. A soft glow illuminated the forest floor below, and in that glow, the shifting, murmuring masses spoke in low tones, creating a buzz, displacing the sounds of the day. The Commodore, poised in the midst of things, was himself surrounded on all sides by querying creatures of every sort. He was an impressive figure indeed, a trusted and capable leader in every apparent way.

"Excuse me!" The Commodore raised his arms to quiet the crowd. "Please, everyone, quiet down!"

There was gradual silence as everyone moved away from him and sat down.

"I've seen you around," Dillon said to Peter, continuing his conversation in a tone suddenly too loud. Peter nodded, a bit uncomfortable with ignoring the call for silence.

"I'm Peter Phye," he said quietly, then held a finger to his lips and turned to listen to the Commodore. Peter never liked to seem impolite.

"I know that," came the assertive reply. "Your name has a pleasing ring to it," Dillon said. "Unlike mine, which is purely descriptive and stumbles from the lips."

"The seed of anxiety has been sown in Efemera," announced the Commodore.

"Who was that big gump that attacked you yesterday?" Dillon asked, still way too loudly. Peter cringed, but was relieved when a second later the crowd buzzed over the Commodore's statement. Peter held a finger to his lips again.

"Sorry," said Dillon.

The Commodore raised his arms and the crowd settled once more as he continued, "As you all know by now..."

"What a disgraceful misuse of fruit," Dillon whispered. "Not t' mention his unkindness towards you."

"Yeah. Please," whispered Peter. "I think we should just listen for now."

Dillon nodded and turned to listen. And, as the Commodore continued, Peter heard a persistent hiss from the trees outside the meeting place, similar to, but somehow less pleasant than that of the wind blowing through the leaves. He looked around, then at Dillon.

"Hobgoblins," whispered Dillon. "Fairies transmuted by opportunity. Weaklin's really, prone t' bad decisions. Nothin' t' be afraid of, though. They can't hurt you. But they will infest both day and night now that they've got the chance. They're the so-called ghosts in the machine... *deus ex machina*... here now t' save the day."

Peter looked hard and saw the glow of eyes from the shadows beyond the meeting place.

"But I wonder who'll save us from *them*?" whispered Dillon into Peter's ear, from where he stood on a branch above Peter's shoulder.

"We have assembled a top corps of sleuths to see what they can find out about this problem we're currently experiencing," said the Commodore. "And they will work in concert with..."

"Problem! That's an understatement!" someone cried out, and the crowd was once again set abuzz.

"Please! Please! Quiet down! Let me turn the floor over to our new intelligence director, Mr. Probus Lucien."

A gray owl, which had thus far stood behind the Commodore with wings folded behind him and his back to the crowd, turned his head suddenly to face everyone with a cold, discerning look, his eyes darting from one to every individual in attendance. All went silent at once with gasps.

"You there!" he said after a good long while.

A chipmunk pointed to himself. "Me?"

"Yeah, you," hooted the owl, aligning his body correctly beneath his head. "What can you tell us?"

"...Nothing," the chipmunk squeaked.

"Nothing."

"N-no, sir... I mean, y-yessir."

"Which is it, chipmunk, yes or no?" Mr. Lucien was very intimidating. Peter found himself, as did everyone else, involuntarily shrinking away.

"N-no sir. I don't know anything," the chipmunk said.

"Are we resorting to martial law?" asked Dillon.

Peter held his finger to his lips and ducked down.

"Who said that!" bellowed Mr. Lucien. "I heard that! I hear everything! I see everything! Nothing escapes me!"

"Except the Maestro!" shouted Dillon.

The crowd gasped again. The owl slowly stepped forward. "Who are you?" he asked with an insidious calmness.

Dillon hopped onto Peter's shoulder. Peter was horrified.

"Dillon Hopper," said Dillon. "Sir!"

"I don't recognize the accent, citizen," said the owl. "Are you some sort of anarchist?"

"No sir," Dillon replied. "But I sure don't like bein' leaned on!"

The owl crouched, ready to spring into flight, when the Commodore stepped forward to stop him.

"Please," the Commodore said, "he's a little..." The Commodore touched a finger to his temple and rolled his eyes in circles.

"I see," said the owl. "Then someone needs to control the idiot."

"Why, I'm no...!"

Peter shoved Dillon into his shirt pocket and covered it with his hand. The crowd was buzzing again, all full of nasty glances in Peter's direction. Peter turned and slipped away. He heard the Commodore's voice fading amid a renewed and growing excitement as he walked into the darkness:

"Now, now, on the lighter side, we have music, and acrobatics by the squirrels coming up a little later, so everybody settle down and

just stay where you are. We have a band I think you've all heard of...
(cheering)... Life Is A Canon... (louder cheering)... to round things
out with their current smash, *Blowing Me Away*. But first, Mr.
Lucien..."

And from the shadows, Peter felt the glowing eyes follow him to
his back porch.

Chapter Seventeen

Late For Matins

The birds, less shaken by the tumult for reasons of their own, were in full song by the time the sun began melting away shadows next morning. The different families tended to find their same places in the trees, and it was for this reason that the Whistlers noticed their own son's tardiness and absences.

Icarus Whistler hurried in with his feathers a mess. His mother nudged Mr. Whistler, watching without turning her head or interrupting their song. Mr. Whistler gave a subtle nod.

"Obviously been out all night, again," she whispered.

"Not now."

"He missed Vespers altogether last night, you know?"

"Not *now!*"

Icarus, fully aware of his conspicuous arrival, found a place high up and as far away from his parents as he could. He knew well his mother's wrathful temperament, and that she might easily break into an embarrassing scold, or dole a slap, right in front of everyone. His father, although far less volatile, was murder just the same with all his tired aphorisms.

So when the first morning service had ended...

"And just who do you think you are?!"

"Sorry," was Icarus's worthless reply.

"Do you have any idea how you make us look? Of how a blue jay is stereotyped in this world?"

"Easy, Vi," Mr. Whistler said.

"No! Not easy! This one comes dragging in whenever he pleases, doing Heaven knows what all night long, and with God knows who! ...Oh, I only hope you haven't been hanging around those cats again! I have ears, you know! I know things, mister, more than you might even care to think!" Mrs. Whistler looked at Mr. Whistler. "Others would think we've never even *tried* to raise a proper bird!" She looked again at her son. "So tell us, what are we supposed to do with you?"

Icarus shrugged and looked down. Mrs. Whistler reached up and pulled his head by the top scruff. "Speak! Don't just stand there shrugging!"

"*Ow!* Cut it out, Ma. This whole singin' thing just ain't me."

"Oh, 'it ain't him.' Did you hear that George? It ain't him! Mr. Hip-Hop doesn't like to sing." Mrs. Whistler shook Icarus's head again, demanding: "And just what is 'you?' ...Huh? ...Huh? Does the world need another loafer? ...Huh? Does the world need another thieving magpie? I don't think so!"

She released him so suddenly that Icarus had to give a quick fluff of his wings to keep from falling backward off his perch.

"Son," said Mr. Whistler in a slow monotone, "your mother is right. If you start hanging out with a bad crowd at your time of life, you'll find it hard later to avoid them. Keep good company, son. Good living promotes good living. You need to straighten up and fly right; be a productive part of our community. You don't want to be remembered as a trouble-maker."

Icarus stood with his head down. "Why not?" he mumbled. "Bein' remembered is bein' remembered."

"What?!" his mother shrieked. "*What?!*"

"I said I can't be in Oblivion if I'm bein' remembered, even if it's for bein' bad."

"Well, looky here, George, we got a philosopher in the family! A regular Soarin Churchyard! Won't we be proud; a future leader of the next avian Reformation. ...Am I funny? He thinks I'm funny, George! Look at 'em smile! He doesn't think this is serious. ...Why, I've got a notion to knock that stupid smirk right off your face, little man! Things are about to change around here! ...Do you hear what I'm saying? ...Do you? ...Speak!"

"Yes, I hear you." Icarus turned then to leave, head still down, more to hide untoward facial expressions than in humility.

"Whoa-whoa, where're you going?" his mother demanded.

"To bed," replied Icarus.

Mr. Whistler sighed and shook his head.

"Oh, no you don't!" began Mrs. Whistler again. "Someone's gonna make a bird of you! You're helping your father. He's not feathering this nest alone anymore! Now get yourself together and get ready to work!"

"*Now?*"

Mrs. Whistler made a fist and shook it in her son's face. Mr. Whistler took him under his wing.

"Yes, son," he said, as they moved away. "Afraid so. You see, the airlane to Oblivion is permeated with good intentions, and the fear of the Creator is glory and splendor... especially your particular creator." Mr. Whistler paused with his eyebrows raised as he looked hard at Icarus, then continued, "A wise man is silent till the right time comes, and the shortest distance between two points is a geodesic..."

And off they flew as Mr. Whistler droned on. Mrs. Whistler looked down at Stevie and smiled fondly.

Chapter Eighteen
A Friend

Peter opened his eyes.

"'Bout time," said Dillon. He sat on the headboard of Peter's bed looking down, smiling as brightly as the sunshine filtering in. "And how'd you sleep last night?"

"Fine... I think," said Peter in a creaky voice as he rubbed his eyes.

"And who's Francine?" Dillon added.

"*What?*" replied Peter, sitting up.

"You were huggin' an' a' sweet-talkin' your pillow till I thought maybe *its* name was Francine." Dillon flicked his eyebrows. Peter turned red. His dreaming had indeed become distressing.

"Just kiddin'," said Dillon, snickering in breathy little wheezes. "Say, nice place y' have here. A little cluttered, though."

"I suppose I'm still confused," said Peter, standing up and scratching his bare stomach. "I half expected it was all a dream."

"Ah well, that seems t' be the order a' things these days," said Dillon, flitting to the window sill and inhaling the outside air deeply. He turned and smiled. "It seems no one knows quite what t' think... or do... since the Maestro's gone missin'."

"I never knew the Queen had an orchestra," said Peter.

"Whose did y' think it was?" asked Dillon.

"I guess I never gave it much thought," replied Peter. He knelt at the sill and leaned on it with two elbows, looking down at Dillon.

"Anyway, they've all been in a dither." said Dillon. "And I hear the Queen's fit t' be tied. Too bad about the Maestro. I really respect him. He's a true professional; only interested in one thing, makin' good music. He's a genius. ...I met him once, y' know. ...Well, didn't actually meet him... but I was nearby while he was meetin' others. Seemed real nice. Knows everything 'bout music. Don't recall him actin' superior. Or anything. Just all business." Dillon studied Peter carefully. "Know what I mean?"

"What? About actin' superior? I never cared what anyone thought. And besides, why should anyone think they were better than someone else?"

Dillon smiled. "Exactly."

Peter stood up and picked his crumpled shorts off the floor. "I've never seen anything like you before," he said as he pulled them on. "Do you live with your family?"

"Got no family," said Dillon. "None in these parts, anyway. I live alone in a little place in the woods not too far from your window. Got a fireplace and a chimney, and a front porch. Real cozy."

Peter pulled a blue T-shirt over his head.

"Nice choice a' color," said Dillon, putting his thumbs in the armholes of what Peter likened to a blue vest and holding it out with a grin.

Peter smiled and smoothed his hair. "You said you were brought here in a jug?"

"That's right," Dillon said. "Shanghaied by a boy I never even saw! He plucked me from a tree branch while I was enjoyin' a meal and tossed me into a plastic jug. *Me*! Of all us eatin' that day, it was *me* got taken away! Hardly seems fair. A couple holes punched in the top, and there I languished for days. No food. No water. Hot sun beatin' down on me. Barely escaped with my life, and would've died if it weren't for his own carelessness. He forgot about me and a coon pulled the cap off in his back yard an' told me t' beat it while I had the chance. Said he wouldn't eat me 'cause I looked too much like a pill he found once that he swore made him rattle when he walked for two straight days. Didn't have t' tell me twice! Quite a shop a' horrors the kid had there. Thought I heard things cryin' out from inside a corn-crib. I tore outta there an' never looked back." Dillon lowered his eyes, "My family's a long ways away. I don't ever expect t' see 'em again. Wouldn't know 'em anyway. I was barely outta the nymph stage when he nabbed me. ...Y' see, I'm different from the others here, and it's hard t' be really happy." Dillon sighed. "I sure do miss my Mama."

He looked away.

"I'm sorry," said Peter.

Dillon nodded with his head down, waving a silent hand at Peter. There were a couple of sniffles. They were quiet for a moment or two, then Peter said, "How about we find the Maestro and make the Queen happy again?"

Dillon looked at Peter, his eyes a little red. "How?" he asked.

"I got an idea," said Peter.

Dillon wiped his eyes.

Chapter Nineteen
Aeolus

"**M**ay we speak to Placido?" asked Dillon, smiling politely.

"Herr Placido does not speak. He sings!"

Dillon's polite smile turned into a sneer. Lankford Palladin, the gaunt leopard frog whom he addressed, was snooty and effete. He raised his chin and threw his shoulders back, along with an upward flourish of his hands as he said the word "sings." Peter and Dillon had found the place where the frogs hung out, and where Herr Placido, first among them, spent his days amongst Lankford and all the other "Water-Lilies," eating himself into a mood of creativity... or, as Dillon put it, "just plain fatness." Peter had suggested, and Dillon agreed, that an interim conductor might help bridge the gap left by the Maestro's absence. Herr Placido seemed a likely first choice, being a primo soloist of outstanding reputation. Peter, in his bourgeois opinion, always considered the frogs to carry the orchestra of the night. Dillon politely informed him that such misconceptions were common among amateurs, and that, sadly, Herr Placido and all the "chirping" Palladins (with crude emphasis on chirping) were of the same opinion, even though their part was virtually unimportant on the grand scale.

"...And he surely will not sing to *you*," finished Palladin flatly. He looked at Peter and Dillon as if smelling something unpleasant, then raised his hands to his chest and whisked them away with his finger-tips. "Now go away. Please," he said, and turned and leapt off in a single bound.

"Why, I'd like to punch that ninny right in the nose!" said Dillon, turning to stare, open-mouthed, at Peter. "Who do they think they are? That big, fat, bag-a'-wind won't even talk to us? I've overlooked the fact he's been slippin'. He's losin' his range. His pitch is way off and he's flat 'cause he can't reach the notes no more. And I'm not the only one who thinks so."

"Maybe if we could talk to him," Peter suggested.

"Oh, but Herr Placido doesn't talk, *he sings!*" said Dillon, flitting into the air.

"C'mon," Peter said. "Let's find him ourselves. He must be here somewhere."

Peter combed the swampy shoreline, his feet squish-squish-squishing, moving the tall weeds aside with a foot every step of the way.

Plop!

"Over there," said Dillon, who stood on Peter's shoulder and pointed. Peter turned and followed the sound, stepping slowly and carefully, looking hard into the weeds.

Plop! Plop!

"Over there, now," said Dillon, pointing behind them.

Peter turned and followed the sound again, moving quicker this time.

Plop!

"Over there," said Dillon.

Peter turned around to follow the sound.

Plop!

"Over there," said Dillon, pointing behind them again.

Peter looked at Dillon, who looked at Peter and shrugged.

"How big is this Herr Placido, anyway?" asked Peter, "I understood him to be quite fat, according to you."

"Oh, he is. Big. *Huge.* Like this." Dillon held his arms out and puffed his cheeks.

"Well then," said Peter, "how could he be here and there so fast?"

Dillon squinted in keen comprehension. "Must be those snotty Palladins, runnin' us around," he said. "Whole family a' nothin's that can't sing a lick, protectin' that fatso from an honest day's work! Let's ignore 'em, and figure the faster they plop, the closer we're gettin'."

Peter moved. There was a *plop* behind him.

"Keep goin' Peter. That way."

There was another *plop* and Peter moved quickly away from it.

Plop! Plop! Plop-plop-plop!

Peter kicked the weeds with his foot.

"*Stop!*" screamed Lankford, flying out of nowhere and landing on Peter's shoe. A gigantic bullfrog was there, just under Peter's foot, brown and round, like a soccer ball, and haughty looking, with his mouth turned down in the corners and a white scarf looped jauntily about his neck.

"You're going to *step* on him!" cried Lankford.

"I see him," said Peter, remarkable for his patience.

"No thanks to you!" added Dillon.

"*He will not talk to you!*" screamed Lankford Palladin, leaping to Herr Placido's side, who stared contemptuously in silence. "I told you he will not talk to you, or anyone else! He must save his golden throat!"

"Herr Placido..." began Peter.

"*Are you insane*?! How *dare* you!" interrupted the mortified Palladin, who appeared for a split second to be faint. "He hates to be addressed directly and does not like even to be looked at! Please! Look away and do not address him! You must communicate through me!"

"'Golden throat.' Why, you overblown... I swear, I'll..."

"Dillon," Peter interrupted, "please, let me."

Dillon looked at Peter, breathing heavily with fists clenched.

"Herr Placido, I'm Peter Phye, and this is Dillon Hopper. We've come to ask a favor of you."

"Ha!" Lankford laughed, "Herr Placido does not grant favors!"

Herr Placido closed his eyes and turned -- slowly, laboriously --

away from Peter.

"Herr Placido," said Peter again, "all I ask is..."

Herr Placido slipped into the water with a heavy *ker-PLUNK!*

"Ha! There is your answer!" exclaimed a triumphant Lankford.

"How rude!" exclaimed Dillon.

"How rude, indeed!" chirped the leopard frog. "How dare you excite him this way!"

"Has he no responsibility to the community that supports him? He's not the bullfrog he was in May no more," replied Dillon.

Lankford Palladin gasped. "Lower your voice!" he said. Then, lowering his own, "Can you do what he does? Can either of you? He has a rare and special talent! I only hope, for your sake, you didn't upset him. He has a very delicate constitution! So help me, if he cannot sing, you'll answer to the Queen!"

"Answer t' the Queen? We're on a mission *for* the Queen, in case y' didn't know. Nobody's been singin'... or haven't you been listenin'?" Dillon glared at Lankford, and Lankford stared back with his mouth agape and eyes wide, obviously taken by Dillon's little embellishment. He couldn't have appeared more stunned had he been slapped across the face, nor could Dillon have been more pleased with the result.

"Herr Placido has not been singing because of creative differences with the orchestra," he answered in a breathy whisper. "And he will remain silent until his demands are met."

Dillon looked at Peter and threw up his hands.

"What demands?" asked Peter.

"The buzzing of the gadflies in the third movement, they are constantly early and in the wrong key," began Lankford, "causing Herr Placido to *appear* to be flat. There was a *hair* in his beverage Tuesday night. He nearly vomited! Herr Placido demands the termination of the shaggy vermin that delivered it, as well as a formal apology from the Maestro, himself! The temperature of the water is unacceptable: he has extremely sensitive skin and is prone to blotching..."

"He thinks the orchestra exists for him. I don't think he even realizes the Maestro is missing," said Peter.

"I don't think he even knows he lives in Efemera!" said Dillon.

"...the percussionists must not detract from Herr Placido's grand entrance into the first movement with their obscene clucking and tapping. ...I mean, *really*, to think the birds, with their..."

"This is pointless," said Dillon. "I..."

Snap! Snap!

Everyone was stopped short by two loud *snaps* from the weeds near where Herr Placido had slipped into the water. Lankford Palladin jumped immediately in response, disappearing into the long grass.

"Now you've done it!" he cried a few seconds later. "You've made him speak! And now he has complaints to lodge against the two of you! You really are in for it now, as if you weren't already in enough trouble from me!"

"Let's go," said Peter.

"Thank you," replied Dillon.

Chapter Twenty
Slow Kel

"On a mission for the Queen.'" Peter almost laughed at that.

"Well, we are, ain't we? ...Whether or not she knows it is a separate matter," replied Dillon. "But I suspect she does. And besides, we may need t' throw some weight around, right? Can't be afraid a' gettin' messy."

Peter shrugged and nodded.

"Can you *believe* that guy, though? He's the only one in Efemera not feelin' his mortality these days," said Dillon, shaking his head.

"He sure did think he was special," Peter agreed. "I never would've imagined him to be that way."

"I think he looked constipated," said Dillon. "Popularity went to his head."

"Well, he is good," said Peter, making his way through a denser portion of trees.

Dillon stared until Peter was forced to look down at him on his wrist.

"Good?" Dillon asked. "*Please*! ...Gonk! Gonk! Gonk! ...There, how's that?"

Peter couldn't help but laugh, though Dillon continued to stare.

"A little weak," Peter goaded. "But not too bad."

They continued on a little farther while Peter snickered and Dillon just stared. The foliage was growing thicker, slapping and scratching and scraping at the two of them now.

"You know," Peter said, more seriously, "the other night, before the music stopped..."

"*Weak?*" interrupted Dillon.

"Well, yeah," Peter said. "You know, Herr Placido has a way of filling the air completely with his sound." He watched Dillon, then added, "But he does have an entire orchestra to support him. ...And anyhow, I was only kidding. Voice isn't a magicada's instrument anyway, is it?"

"...Well sure," Dillon said, "I know that. It was just an imitation... you know, a silly imitation t' make a point. I wasn't really *tryin'* or anything... 'cept t' look stupid, that is... just emphasizin' how stupid everybody is t' think that's such a special noise. ...I mean, by golly, we should revere such a jerk 'cause he can make an odd sound?"

"A *nice* sound," said Peter.

"That's open to interpretation," replied Dillon. "Betcha didn't know that when I play diddley-bow you can hear it a mile away."

"That right?"

"Sure is."

Peter whistled, more the type of whistle to denote being impressed than to impress anyone.

"Hey," said Dillon, "that wasn't so bad either. Nice pitch."

"That?"

"Yeah, really. I'm not kiddin'. Any sound has the capability of bein' musical. You got a real knack there."

"Nah," said Peter.

They were silent for a few minutes as they worked their way through the trees. It seemed more and more another bad choice of routes for Peter. He had to take great care to avoid having Dillon swiped from his wrist by branches as he labored through; the cracking of twigs and rustle of leaves being the only sounds heard throughout the otherwise quiet woodland. Dillon, for his part, was as busy as Peter, ducking and swatting. And grumbling.

"Could we have found a more tangled route?"

Peter didn't answer, but began instead to quietly whistle *Yankee-Doodle Dandy* to himself, a ditty he'd been fond of since the Fourth of July concert in the county park near Idlewild.

"Um-hm, um-hm, there y' go!" declared Dillon, "Carryin' a tune, as well!"

"Nah," replied Peter, waving modestly but smiling receptively. Then he started disassembling the melodic theme into a sort of cadenza (a la Wolfgang Mozart's *Twinkle, Twinkle, Little Star*, which he'd heard as well, but not at the county park). But he'd gone too far... at least that was one way to interpret Dillon's sudden and conspicuous lack of enthusiasm. Peter snuck a couple looks to gauge the effectiveness of his little musical aggrandizement, and Dillon just smiled and nodded politely. Peter tried a little harder for awhile -- until he started to stumble, musically speaking – then just rounded it out and decided to leave it at that. Ah well, he thought, better to say nothing at all, as they say. That was the polite thing, which reminded him...

"You know," he said. "Can I say something without you takin' it wrong?"

"Sure, buddy, say anything y' like."

"Well..." Peter began, clear now of the branches and within sight of his house, "you're really a very nice guy..."

Peter paused. A silence settled.

"Ah, well," interceded a smiling Dillon, bursting with unspoken sentiment. "I think I understand what you're tryin' t' say, and I thank y' kindly for the compliment. And, by the way, no need t' be so bashful around me about showin' a little love." Dillon nudged Peter affectionately. "I've always thought a' myself as a bit of a sucker when it comes t' camaraderie and the whole esprit de corpse..."

"But I think it would help you a lot more to make friends if you weren't so quick to blow... you know, your temper. And I don't think you should call the other animals names," blurted Peter, before Dillon, whose mouth was hanging open, could finish what he'd begun to say.

Dillon closed his mouth, then asked calmly, "I wasn't feelin' your musical whirlwind enough, is that it?"

"What?"

"No disrespect intended," Dillon said. "You're new to it, is all. Your approach t' musical trainin' should be in smaller bites, I'd say. Otherwise y' learn t' be a noise-maker and not a musician, and y' don't wanna be a noise-maker, do ya?"

"No," said Peter. "And forget about that. I got carried away. Just a little musical joke, is all. ...Like what you were doin'."

Dillon eyed him suspiciously for a few seconds.

"Whirlwind", Peter repeated thoughtfully. "I suppose that's the word for it."

"So you think I blow and call the other animals names?"

"Sometimes," said Peter.

"Me?"

"Um-hm. Some of the others might treat you better if you were more approachable... you know, if you gave 'em a chance to get to know you."

Dillon stared quietly for a few seconds, as if assimilating the suggestion, then shrugged. "Nah, don't you believe it. And don't think I haven't tried. Tryin' t' be friendly landed me a role as lackey servant to a superstar acrobat one time... till I finally told 'em t' bust his own nuts. I'm a magicada in a world full a' bugs. They don't like me, so I don't like them."

Dillon folded his arms and turned and looked ahead. Peter stopped again.

"You can't say that for sure," he said. "You could stand to be a bit friendlier, even when things don't go your way; that's all I'm sayin'."

"Well, my Mama had quite a temper, and..." Dillon stopped and looked across the back yard as they were nearly out of the woods. "Wait a minute," he said, and flew from Peter's hand. He fluttered in a high arc and landed across the yard in the grass alongside a turtle, which Peter suddenly noticed as well, looking around with his neck fully extended.

"Hey, Kel."

The turtle blinked slowly.

"Hel-low, Dillon," he replied in a very slow voice.

"Where y' goin', Kel?"

"To the beach. Wanna come?"

"Nah. You know, me and water."

Kel smiled. "*Huh-Huh-Huh*, Don't like water much, do you?"

"Nah," said Dillon. "Say, Kel, the beach is that way, y' know? You're goin' the wrong way."

Kel blinked. "No," he said, "it's towards that tree. Same direction I always go. I look up every now and then to keep my bearings."

"Uh-uh, Kel." Dillon shook his head and pointed behind him. "Look, there's the tree y' want. Over there."

"Are you sure?" Kel asked. "They sure look alike." He squinted with uncertainty.

"From the ground they do. But trust me, I'm right."

Kel lowered his head and began to turn his body. "Well whatta ya know," he said.

"Yeah, gotta watch that, Kel. That tree you're headed for, it's across the road. Y' manage t' get over it without gettin' flattened and you'll be in the Deepest Forest. Go there, and you may never find your way back."

"Gee whiz, and I was sure... Whoops!" Kel disappeared with blinding speed into his shell.

"Oh boy!" cried a breathless Peter as he ran up. "Do you know him?!" He stopped and knelt beside them. "I find him in my back yard all the time."

"Yeah, his name's Kel. I think you scared the do-do outta him, though. Come on out, Kel. This is my friend, Peter. He won't hurt you." Dillon looked patiently at Peter as he spoke to Kel. "He's headed for the beach... you know, the pond... and he's lost again. ...Come on out, Kel. Meet my friend."

Kel's head began to emerge.

"Kel, this is Peter."

"Hello, Kel," said Peter with an eager smile.

Kel just stared and blinked.

"He's actually hilarious," said Dillon. "He does pantomime. ...Kel, show Peter some a' your stuff."

Kel remained wary.

"Go on, Kel. He's my friend. He'll get a big laugh."

Kel emerged fully from his shell and stood upright on his back legs, pretending to pull himself there by an invisible rope.

Dillon laughed. "Look at that, Peter! This guy really cracks me up!"

Peter laughed, and Kel pretended to lower himself down by the same rope. He was good, and made himself appear to be actually descending in small increments. Then he pretended to suddenly find himself locked in a box of glass, feeling the walls and ceiling with probing palms and an anxious expression, mouth open, shaped like the letter O.

Dillon laughed, "Kel, you are a hoot!"

Dillon looked at Peter, who was laughing as hard as he was. Kel stopped and smiled, and nodded his head, then put a thumb in his mouth and tipped his head back. Peter laughed as he watched Kel's Adam's apple bob. Dillon's laughter slowed. Then Kel lowered his thumb and staggered in circles before spinning on his tail several times and falling flat on his back, wobbling around on his shell like a saucer set down too hard. He lay there with his eyes closed, mouth open, and tongue sticking out to the side.

Dillon had stopped laughing, and looked at Peter, who still thought it was all tremendously funny, laughing and slapping his thigh.

"Ohh--*kay*, Kel, that's enough. Peter, let's help 'em t' the beach."

"Whoa, whoa! Wait a minute," Peter said. "Not yet. Let's just see a little more. Kel, you're a riot!"

Kel raised his head and smiled over the top of the bottom of his shell, that alone causing Peter to break again into hysterics.

"No, Peter, I think that's enough," said Dillon. "We got work t' do. C'mon Kel, cut it out."

Kel smirked at Dillon, who shook his head, annoyed, then looked at Peter. "C'mon, Peter, time for Kel t' go. I'll catch y' later, Kel." Dillon leaned toward him, "Um-um-um," he whispered, "you went too far. I told you he was my friend."

Chapter Twenty-one

Deus Ex Machina

Peter carried Kel to the pond and placed him in the water. Kel said, "Thank you," and Peter said, "Anytime," and Dillon told Peter that if he ever saw Kel again it most likely meant he was lost and to "just toss him back, quickly." Kel and Peter both laughed at that, but not Dillon, who told Peter he was serious. "I mean it," he said, "just toss him back. ...Quickly."

With that done, there was little else to do, other than circumscribe the pond, which Peter did, meandering through the trees with Dillon on his shoulder, waiting for ideas to come to him. A dearth of ideas and the scourge of tedium suddenly loomed large. Peter would rather have been entertained by Kel a while longer, but Dillon had been so insistent on placing him in the water that Peter figured it was for Kel's own well-being that it be done so quickly. He wouldn't have wanted to see him get flattened on the dirt road, or lost in the Deepest Forest.

"What's the matter," Peter asked after awhile. "Would he have dried up or something if we hadn't put him in the water?"

Dillon just looked like he wasn't sure what Peter had meant.

"Kel, I mean," prompted Peter.

"Somethin' like that," Dillon answered.

Peter nodded as if he understood. He wouldn't want that to happen, either. He started thinking again about Kel's quirky little performance when another thought came.

"That was the oddest thing I ever saw," he said. "Now that I think of it."

It was the cheekiness he was referring to that struck him as odd. That sort of humor was new to him.

"He gets carried away," said Dillon.

Peter laughed. "If I didn't know better, I'd say..."

"Don't try to assign any meanin' t' anything he does," Dillon said. "He's just a clown." Then he said, just quietly enough for Peter not to hear, "Jus' not as slow as some think."

It *did* seem vaguely familiar. But no matter, Peter supposed, because what would a turtle know anyhow? The two walked on. With Kel gone and the day beginning to drag, Peter had taken to thinking about a certain something else, something he figured he must be relating to Kel's performance sheerly due to the time of day... an estimation due in some part, no doubt, to Dillon's curt and well-intended (if not altogether truthful) reassurances, and Peter's trust in them. And here was the thing: the lunch hour normally brought a lingering thought, a thought that nagged and prodded; a thought that could only be pushed aside for so long; and the fact that Peter could relate this thought to Kel's farce was proof enough to him of a logical and natural juxtaposability of seemingly disparate and absurd circumstances in his life: In this case, his mother. There was an interconnectedness of things in life, even absurd things, and one could reconcile innumerable things if they were clever enough; one need only be clever enough. Peter imagined he was just realizing this.

"How's it possible that Efemera can exist without people knowing it?" he asked.

"Some people know it," Dillon said.

"Who?"

"Efemera's an enchantment, a moment ordinary people usually find unexpectedly or in hindsight," answered Dillon. "Most folks pass right through it and never even notice... not astute enough. The more intelligent one is, y' see, the more things a' rarity they find, put so eloquently by Soarin Churchyard, the only bird I ever met worth a hoot or a whistle." Dillon paused as he gave consideration to his next thought. "This is our home though, the others and I. You know: us lesser creatures. We've always consorted as friends with the means to our end and never given it a single thought, till lately. Now the cattle don't graze so peacefully anymore."

Ah, and there it was again, the juxtaposing of incongruities; the placing side-by-side of things that didn't seem to belong together. Although the process must have existed legitimately all along, Peter suddenly noticed himself seeing it with so much clarity wherever he chose to look. And why not, there was no law he'd ever heard of to forbid some subtle harmony between apparent unlikely-hoods. His former prejudice against it seemed more a self-imposed limitation than anything else... either that or a defect in his learning. The problem, Peter suspected, was to *expect* this "subtle harmony" to be accessible for one to put their finger on, and that was tricky, because one could easily confuse logic for harmony that way. Logic, as Peter knew it, was the answer to a math problem. But there was more to life than that. Heck, in more general terms he'd already concluded that one might not even find the "subtle harmony" to be logical at all. It might be completely unpredictable, like the harmony that comforted him when listening to falling rain. But more likely it was totally incomprehensible. Peter wrangled with that in terms of his mother. In fact, Dillon was sounding a bit like Peter's father, and, although not meant by Dillon as metaphors, Peter recognized the similarities in the things they were saying, and found himself suddenly grasping their meanings quite well.

"I don't think of you as lesser," he said, breaking a dead twig from a tree branch as he passed.

"Eh," Dillon flung his hand in the air.

"Anyway," Peter said, "why hide it?"

"What, this place? It's not hidden, really. Y' see, you can make a person believe by showin 'em, or they can find it on their own."

Peter rolled the twig between his fingers. "And which is better?"

"Dunno," answered Dillon. "Not for me t' say. It's our choices that make us what we are."

"What about me?" asked Peter.

Dillon smiled. "All I do know, is that now you're here, you'll eventually have t' go."

They stopped at a clearing along the edge of the pond, on the shore across from where the meeting place had been. The ground was soft and spongy beneath the leaves, which acted as a cushion to keep it from becoming wet. The ground gave with each of Peter's steps. He stopped and shifted his weight from left to right several times to test it, then knelt. The two were silent as they looked around. Heat and humidity had dragged things to a virtual standstill, as well as limited the possibilities. There would certainly be no running, jumping or climbing. Peter wiped his forehead with the tail of his shirt.

"Hot," he said.

"That's for sure," answered Dillon. He began to quietly blow an unfamiliar melody through his lips as he patted around the outside of his vest with two hands.

Peter tossed away the twig he'd been holding, noticing things had suddenly grown very quiet. It was getting close to lunchtime. He thought about his house and of his mother. "What's that you're singin'?" he asked.

"Oh, nothin', Dillon answered. "Just a little somethin' I been workin' on."

Peter threw his head back and rubbed his neck, then stopped to look into the trees. Dillon stopped patting his vest and snapped his fingers as if realizing he'd forgotten something. "Darn it."

"What's that?" Peter asked at the same time.

"What?"

"That. ...There." Peter pointed to a tree whose leaves were alternate shades of dull and shiny green as they hung limp in the heavy air.

"Where?" asked Dillon.

Peter turned sideways to point. Dillon looked down his arm and forefinger, crouched, with one eye closed, as if looking down a gun barrel.

"Above the branch closest to the ground," Peter said, stretching his arm.

"I see 'em. Just another fairy." Dillon stood up and opened his eye.

"Is it following us?" asked Peter. "I've been seein' it around."

"Who cares?" Dillon said. "They're pests."

Peter walked slowly to the tree.

"Whatta y' doin', Peter? For cripe's sake, it's just another fairy."

Peter took a deep breath. "He smells like lilacs."

Dillon rolled his eyes.

"I haven't actually met one yet," said Peter.

"Whatta y' mean, they're everywhere."

Peter slowed to a stop. "I've seen lots of everything else, but not fairies," he whispered, his eyes steadily fixed on the fairy. "It *is* a boy, isn't it?"

"That's not an issue with them," answered Dillon impatiently.

The fairy didn't move, but watched carefully. Peter moved closer ...and it vanished. Peter stood and looked at Dillon.

"A quark," said Dillon. "Thought so when I smelled the lilacs."

"A quark?"

"Um-hm."

"Where'd he go?"

"Could be just about anywhere," said Dillon. "Quarks are an odd breed... don't abide by the rules. Wonder what he's doin' here? ...Say, if y' catch him, he'll grant 'cha wishes."

"That's not necessarily true," a voice said, a male voice, speaking with effeminately perfect elocution.

The fairy appeared on Peter's other shoulder, opposite Dillon.

"Hey," said Peter, "don't go away again."

"I have to like you, first," said the fairy. "And quark is a very derogatory term," he said to Dillon, then disappeared again.

"Where are you?" asked Peter.

"Have to keep moving," the fairy's voice said.

"Are you following us," Peter asked, looking around.

"Of course he is," said Dillon. "I told you, they're pests."

"I can help you," the fairy said, reappearing in the air in front of

Peter.

"You?" Dillon asked. "You're a quark."

"Stop it, Dillon, he said that wasn't nice. ...I'm Peter Phye, and this is Dillon Hopper, from the Deep South."

"Miss Shapenchance, at your service," the fairy said. "We met the other night."

Dillon let out a giggle.

"*Miss* Shapenchance?" asked Peter, looking from the fairy to Dillon.

"Miss is my first name. Shapenchance, my last. It's the name given to me by another. I had no say in it."

"Are you sure it doesn't mean you're really a girl?" asked Dillon, still giggling.

"Stop that, Dillon," scolded Peter.

"I prefer Chance, though," the quark said to Peter. Then, turning to Dillon, "And that's not nice. You sound very unkind."

"Hah!" Dillon laughed. "There y' go, quark! Miss Shapen-chance-Call-Me-Chance!"

"Do you *mind?*" Chance asked impatiently. "Just because you don't understand..."

"And who would trust a quark?" interrupted Dillon.

"Hmph!" replied Chance, turning to Peter.

"Why are you so mean to him?" Peter asked.

Dillon's smile faded. "I told you, they're useless."

"That's not true," said Chance to Peter. "They need me, and they know it."

"Oh, is that right?" asked Dillon. "And in what way?"

Chance appeared in front of Dillon. "*Please*, what would you be without me?" he asked. "Hmm? All dullness and mediocrity. A slovenly horde of beasts, that's what. I keep the world turning, literally. I give it its color and flavor. I mix it up for you. Creativity. I propel one beyond mere existence."

"Oh, I hadn't noticed."

"Well, maybe not *you*, and I'm not surprised."

"Oh, no, no, no. I think you need us way more than we need you," said Dillon, pointing a finger at Chance. "Without us, your endless existence would be pointless! You like to play with us. In fact..."

"Please! Stop!" Peter interrupted. "Is there anything wrong with sayin' we all need one another?"

Dillon and Chance crossed their arms and looked away from one another.

"Don't we all want the music restored?" Peter asked.

He waited.

"Fine," said Chance.

"Fine, then," said Dillon, and they touched hands quickly then turned away again, scowling in opposite directions.

"Now," said Peter, "you said you could help us. How?"

"With magic, of course."

Dillon rolled his eyes.

Chapter Twenty-two
The Beehive

There was a clatter through the branches and leaves of the trees, then the *thud-thud* of a rock bouncing on the soft ground near where Peter and Dillon stood by Chance. Peter heard someone talking. Chance vanished. Dillon began nodding his head, pointing a finger in the air and saying:

"*Um-um-um*. Well ain't that somethin'. *Poof!* Just like that and we lose our magician. Ah well, easy come and easy go... lest you'd believed it was magic in the air. And that's about the way it always is with his sort, sorry t' say; irresponsible and self-centered. What made him think we *wanted* his help anyway? Very presumptuous. Um-um-um. No sir, won't pine for his loss none: fact I'd say what we were smellin' wasn't lilacs at all, more like what the ol' Leddy Irons lets loose in the field when he raises his tail, jus' cleverly disguised horse..."

"*Shh!*" said Peter, distracted and looking frightened to death. He recognized the voice. He dropped to his hands and knees and crawled through the brush. He paused as he looked and listened. ...Impish laughter. He craned his neck and held his breath. Sure enough, it was Pixie Anderson, down the shoreline a way with Rex, dressed in oversized cargo shorts that hung so low on his hips they looked like they might have fallen halfway down. And there were his fat, dirty toes, sticking out every which way from a pair of sandals.

"Get over here!" Pixie snarled, pointing to the ground next to him. Rex slowly obeyed, head down, ears back, and tail tucked between his legs. Pixie smacked him on the nose when he finally sat, then pulled up his shorts. Rex looked up with deceptively sad eyes; he was a Rottweiler, fully capable of all the malice his master could teach him, merely beaten down and submissive in his role as pupil. "Fetch!" Pixie heaved a stick into the pickers and caught his shorts again.

Rex looked, moved a few hesitant steps, then stopped and sat.

"*Fetch*, you stupid idiot!"

Rex stared down.

"*Git!*" Pixie walked up and kicked him in the rear end.

"What kinda monster is that?" whispered Dillon.

"Pixie Anderson," whispered Peter.

"How appropriate," said Dillon. "I'm surprised the fairies let 'em get away with that."

"Well," whispered Peter, "the dog's no peach, either. He acts just like Pixie to everyone except Pixie."

Pixie lobbed a rock into the pickers. Rex yelped.

"Ooohh, I'm gonna be sick," said Dillon. "I can't watch any more. Let's go."

Pixie laughed unnecessarily loudly, then threw another rock into the trees above them.

"Wait, not yet!" Peter whispered. "He might see us."

"Oh, cool!" Pixie yelled. He threw another rock, then another. Peter and Dillon looked up.

"He's throwin' at that bees nest," whispered Dillon, pointing up. "I'll be right back."

And he flew away.

Pixie threw a steady barrage of stones, snatching at his falling shorts with the completion of every effort. And when he tired of rocks, he chose a long stick and hurled it with a baseball swing to better effect. It twirled like a propeller on its way through the leaves and caused the branch with the hive to jar and shake just a bit. Pixie watched hopefully for a second or two, then bunched his baggy shorts in one fist and poked around some more on the ground. Peter watched as bees began to trickle out of the hive. Pixie popped up and tried again with another curved, knotty stick. He twisted then uncoiled his torso violently, and flung it, *whoop-whoop-whooping* in the air so it struck the branch clean and hard. He waited again with an open-mouthed stare, but either didn't notice or wasn't impressed by the wisp of bees beginning to swirl about. He leaned over and tugged and tugged on the end of a branch sticking out from the leaves like a lever, but it kept on wanting to pull out from somewhere deep beneath the ground, six feet and more behind him. His heaving left the ground behind him looking like a great, surging worm was rearing up between his legs, and then diving away every time he leaned back and had at it. He jerked and jerked and then started stomping near its base to break it off to a manageable length. Peter watched the bees pile out like a torrent of angry black smoke. Pixie, who'd become carelessly absorbed in uncovering and busting off useable segments of the branch, was bent over, rooting beneath the leaves with his hands, when the first of the bees crawled down his boxers and stung him somewhere in the nether region between their elastic waistband and the top of his sagging shorts, a considerable distance by bee standards, which included most of his bare buttocks. Pixie shrieked and jerked and reared around as if he'd been jabbed with a cattle prod, and then looked up all wild and confused. And before he could even comprehend what had hit him, he was inundated with bees. Off he ran, cavorting like a smoldering marionette, hands flying between holding his drawers up and flailing wildly about, squealing and screaming and slapping at himself, hitting the ground in sporadic barrel rolls and popping up again as Rex hurried to follow, barking fiercely all the way.

Peter stood up when they were gone. Dillon returned a few seconds later and landed on his shoulder, bearing a somewhat wicked smile, and with this to say: "Bees, meet Pixie Anderson. Pixie Anderson: bees."

Chapter Twenty-three
The Tittering Annuals

Peter was bound for his house, with each approaching step stirring in him an ever-increasing sense of dread. He crossed his back yard with Dillon on his shoulder, toward the porch, which was wet beneath two flower boxes newly placed there. The brilliant flowers they held were the one thing Peter's mother seemed to take an avid interest in. Peter liked them, too, making them, perhaps, the only thing they had in common.

But Peter thought to himself that they didn't belong there. He wondered what mood his mother was in, and why she had put them there. He wondered if he should dare bring Dillon into the house, a thought that made him want to turn and run the other way... his mother but a noxious thought he wished to hide from. But, it was lunchtime and he really had no place else to go, hungry, and in such heat.

Peter thought these things as he drew nearer, but was distracted, and slowed his pace.

"...No, it's definitely you!" a voice was saying, along with others all at once; and all sounding as if they had inhaled Helium from balloons.

"...Yes, I think she is jealous..."

"...It appears the sun shines only for you..."

"...You haven't aged a day since I first saw you..."

"...No, no, no! Not wrinkles...!"

"...But I really mean what I say..."

There were coquettish giggles in response.

The voices -- as well as the giggles -- came from the flower boxes. Peter stepped closer to watch as tiny fairies, no bigger than bees (and the careless observer might easily have confused them for bees), hovered and lavished the tittering annuals with insipid flattery.

"What are they doing?" Peter asked, jarring Dillon, who look-ed up, confused, having been busily searching again through his vest pockets.

"Who?"

"There, on the porch. What're they doing?" Peter pointed to the flowers, and the fairies hovering among them.

"Flowers," Dillon said, somewhat vexed. "Doing exactly what they're supposed to do: nothing." He looked down again and muttered into his vest.

The pansies gawked gloriously at Peter, with their whining, bawling expressions, while the fairies continued to lavish transparent nothingness.

There was a quiet *pop* in the air above Peter's shoulder, opposite Dillon, who quickly closed his vest to look up at the same time as Peter. A small black ellipse opened in the air. Chance climbed through, backwards, then closed the hole in a zipping fashion, from bottom to top. Heat and a lot of static noise escaped from the hole before he was done closing it.

"Our quark friend is back," sang Dillon in a musical voice, followed by a pointed, "But not so grand an entrance this time."

"What's in there," asked Peter, trying to ignore Dillon and hoping Chance would do the same.

"It's very crowded," Chance replied, alighting on Peter's shoulder and straightening his white tunic, now adorned with many and variously colored flowing scarves, reminding Peter of the flowers themselves. "They're nurturing them," he said. "The flowers. That's what keeps them blooming. They need a lot of attention."

"And lots of everything else," remarked Dillon. "Very little return for the investment, if you ask me. They're useless. Don't even bear fruit."

"They're not supposed to," replied Chance. "That's not their purpose."

Dillon pulled down on his vest from the bottom with two hands to straighten it. "But look at 'em," he said. "They're pitiful. Even the withered ones think they're beautiful. And the buds, barely unfurled, think they're more unique in some way than all the others before 'em."

Chance looked patiently at Dillon in a way that may have seemed a bit condescending. "They are simply meant to put a smile on everyone's face," he said. "That's all. That's their purpose, and I think they do a fine job of it." Chance smiled as he watched. "Aren't they magnificent?" he said. "Each individual so similarly beautiful, yet unique at the same time." He looked again at Dillon. "The fairies don't mind nurturing them, so I think it works for everyone."

"They make my mom happy," said Peter, sitting with a heavy sigh on the porch between the flower boxes.

"Hmph!" replied Dillon, "Not me."

Peter leaned down and sniffed the flowers in one of the boxes, the smell unexpectedly reminding him of the day before, when in the meadow Pixie Anderson had pushed his face into the grass. Peter sighed again and withdrew, unhappy with that association.

"I could care less," continued Dillon. "But it's nice t' know there's a purpose to it, 'cause I was beginnin' t' think '*The Creator*' was purely idlin' away in boredom."

Chance shook his head, again in what might have seemed a condescending way, and Dillon stuck his tongue out at him.

"Where do you go when you disappear?" Peter asked.

"To work," replied Chance, interrupting his stunned stare at Dillon to look at Peter.

"Work?"

"We must all have something to do."

"And what kind of work do you do?"

"That's hard to explain," said Chance.

"Oh please, do try," said Dillon. "We have time."

"Ah, and the disenfranchised musician has unwittingly touched on it. Time is yours, not mine. I visit here, but really belong to another place."

Dillon nudged Peter on the neck, reminding Peter that he had noticed Dillon become somewhat... competitive. And that was a word for it. Dillon had no intention of leaving his newfound boon companion to the likes of whimsical Chance. For one, Dillon's own past and present were so tightly approximated between the opening and nearly simultaneous closing of the door to his future that true friendship was a once in a lifetime rarity. True friendship was a rarity under any circumstance. Peter knew this intuitively as well, although we mustn't say he'd ever elaborated on it to any great extent before. But there was another, nobler reason for Dillon's apparent competitiveness, more deeply seated and perhaps deservedly come by: a perception on his part of being, thus far, somehow wronged by Chance. The wilds of Efemera were filled with unsavory characters, as Dillon was in a better position to know. Chance was an altogether new creature to Peter, heretofore only hazy and speculative in nature -- as are many things to a boy of twelve -- and Dillon felt a duty to dissuade his newfound and naïve companion from cavorting with the wrong sorts, or, if not that, then at least to not mistake their smiling indifference for friendship. Peter, though, for his part, was surprisingly subtle in his untwisting of these touchy little strands.

"Stop, Dillon," was all Peter said, trying not to sound irritated as he itched his neck. "Let him talk." He looked again at Chance. "The Forever?"

Dillon's eyes popped open wide and he leaned forward.

"No," said Chance. "Actually, I live in a Realm of Possibility. But I can get to The Forever from there, and anywhere else." He leaned forward, then whispered, "I'm the ghost in the machine," then winked at Dillon, who jumped with a start and leaned back to assume a barely convincing look of disinterest. Chance leaned again into Peter's ear and whispered for a few seconds more, then vanished. Peter looked quickly from Dillon to the fairies buzzing amongst the annuals.

"And?" Dillon asked.

He waited.

"Well?" he said. "What the heck was that he whispered t' you?"

"Nothing," said Peter.

"Come on."

"Nothing."

"He said *somethin'*, I heard him whisperin'."

"Nothing," Peter said. "Don't worry about it."

"Who's worried? I just wondered what he said, is all. I thought we were friends. But that's all right, you go on and keep your little secrets."

"It's not a secret," said Peter, exasperated. "Don't worry about it. ...Ah, gee whiz, I'll tell y' later, all right?"

"Sure y' will," said Dillon.

"Really," said Peter. "I will."

"Well, maybe I won't be interested later. Maybe I'm not interested now."

And with that, Dillon began a silent sulk.

Chapter Twenty-four

Laestrygonians

"I'm hungry," said Peter, eventually breaking a cool five minute silence.

It was very hot and sunny otherwise. Peter leaned forward with his head between his knees, still afraid to go inside. He was throwing a shadow on Dillon, who sweltered on the step below, dabbing his forehead with the back of a hand.

"It's a hundred degrees in the shade," puffed Dillon.

It was quite a warm spell, the warmest in Peter's lifetime, although he was unaware of it. He leaned back on his hands. The cement was hot, so he slumped forward again a few seconds later and looked at his palms, stippled red from the grainy surface of the porch. He watched as a mosquito hovered, and then landed on his forearm with such single-minded determination that it might just as well have been landing on a whole other planet... albeit a planet with the capability of slapping you dead the minute you arrived. Peter thought it odd that a mosquito would find him at all in the broad, hot daylight, as well as that anything could be so driven by proclivity that it wouldn't recognize – or at least acknowledge – the danger. He decided to test his own self-control by not reacting. He watched as the mosquito jockeyed for a purchase and then pierced his skin in as unbothered and prosaic a manner as ever there was or might conceivably be. The mosquito swelled... swelled... swelled... and then bobbed away like a fighter jet off an aircraft carrier, weighed down heavily with its cache of Phye blood.

"Y' lookin' for a case a' the scrilly-scratchies?" Dillon asked. Peter was suddenly aware that he'd been watching the whole time. "Don't let 'em do that," Dillon added. "They're filthy, flittin' from this one t' that one, passin' on who-knows-what all along the way."

"I know," Peter said, scratching at the reddening weal on his forearm. "It'll itch all week. I almost gave myself an infection once, scratchin' so hard."

Two more mosquitoes found his arm, and Peter slapped them. "Whatta y' like to eat?" he asked, standing up and flicking a few pieces of grit from his palm.

"Thought I had a straw here," said Dillon, tapping his vest again for the umpteenth time, when at last it finally came to him: "Shoot!" (He'd snapped it in a mishap at dinner the night before, during a row with someone over "proper ambiance." Dillon knew better than to hold anything of value between his hands while under the sort of emotional strain quarreling with jerks causes, but this one had gotten the better of him.)

"I'll need a new one," he said to Peter. "I usually just stick it in a branch and drink."

("Jerk," by the way, was Dillon's term to describe his opponent in this aforementioned fray while, in all fairness, a certain degree of empathy might have been in order for both parties, since straws, as nearly everyone knows, while being magnificently sonorous to their owners, can often be unpleasant for others to listen to.)

Peter said, "We can get something from in the house."

He held out his hand, and Dillon hopped onto the back of it. Peter eased the creaky old screen door open, stepped into the house, then shut it again just as carefully. It was quiet inside, no sign of his mother. He pulled gently on the refrigerator door. It popped open to the quiet clatter of bottles inside. Peter cringed at the mere thought of the prospective crisis such unobtrusive noises might provoke, his mother's eyes snapping open wherever she lay.

"*Phew*! Whatta y' keep in there?" Dillon asked. "Smells like a mulch pile."

"Food," whispered Peter. "*Shh*."

"Food for *who*?" Dillon waved a hand back and forth in front of his nose. "It don't smell very fresh."

Peter had always known himself the fridge smelled funny -- just like the rest of his house -- but being so common a thing, he never gave it much thought. But now that he thought about it, a stinky house was no joke! And here's what else he thought: it was *embarrassing*! He was actually embarrassed to have anyone over. ...Which was one of the reasons he always lost contact with his schoolmates on weekends and breaks -- like Roland Plessinger – all because his house stunk! And because his house stunk, Peter was a boy without a clique, an unwitting wraith who floated between cliques – *persona non grata*, as it were -- because without a clique a boy was nothing, virtually non-existent, fodder for any and every other faction that abounded -- and all factions abounded, believe you me, even within humble little agrarian societies -- and if someone like Dillon had noticed the smell then surely anyone else might; just that Dillon was honest enough -- incapable of less, apparently – to say so.

"Wow! And that light stays on all the time? Seems like a waste," Dillon said.

"I don't think the light stays on," whispered Peter. "It switches off when the door closes. ...And you gotta be more quiet. Please. You'll wake up my mom."

"Sorry," replied Dillon softly. "...Bet it doesn't," he whispered.

"Yes it does," said Peter.

"Shut me in there and I'll see for myself." Dillon fluttered onto one of the shelves and stood inside. "Go on," he said through a pinched nose. "Close the door. ...But only for a second."

Peter closed the door and counted to five, then opened it again. Dillon came flying out.

"You wouldn't *believe* the things that live in there!"

"Like what?" asked a wide-eyed Peter.

"It's disgusting!"

"*What?*"

"If I told you, you might never eat again." Dillon threw his tongue out and his eyes watered. "Soon as you shut the door... *boom!...* here they come! Get me outta here!" Dillon motioned for Peter to close the door, cringing and turning his head away. "Go on," he said, "shut it, quick!"

"What comes out?" asked Peter as he held the door, suddenly more annoyed again than alarmed.

"Never mind," said Dillon, "I'll just eat outside." And then adding, just barely loud enough to hear, "And maybe I'll tell *you* later."

Peter, who'd begun an inventory of the refrigerator's contents, halted with the door handle in hand, stooped over and looking in, the "oo" of Dillon's "you" reverberating as far as his own lips, while that sneaky, last little jab ricocheted in his head like a bullet in a Wild West shootout. He collected himself and responded with equal subtleness.

"Quite a little performance," he said, more quietly than Dillon, while slowly closing the door and watching for the light to switch off through a crack.

"Beg pardon?" said Dillon.

"Oh, nothin'."

"No, seriously, I couldn't hear you," said Dillon.

"Did the light stay on?"

Dillon looked at Peter for a second then smiled.

"Yeah, it sure did."

"I don't believe you," Peter said. He stood up and pushed the door shut.

Dillon shrugged.

"Neither of us knows what's in here," Peter said, opening and looking inside the freezer.

Dillon seemed intrigued by the cold mist that swirled out. "Now that's cold," he said. "Must be what winter's like, huh?"

"Um-hm, frozen solid," Peter said, looking in and enjoying the coldness on his skin. "Sometimes it's pretty. Sometimes it's fun. But mostly it's just cold and dark. The lack of sunlight's the worst part; that and the cold or flu everyone's trying t' pass you. Even when the sun does shine, it doesn't shine very long, and you can't imagine how... *HUH!*"

The freezer door was torn from Peter's grip and slammed shut before he could finish what he was saying. Mrs. Phye had appeared from nowhere, shoving it and nearly catching him in the head with it.

"I've told you not to let the cold out!"

"Ah... Well... Ah... What's for lunch?" Peter asked, innocently assessing his mother in too obvious a way. It didn't help that he'd been thinking of her in terms of his newfound enlightenment, the one that he imagined lent harmony and civility to chaos and spoke of the interconnectedness of innumerable absurdities. Staring at her now, all Peter could do was sense that his enlightenment was still lacking in some key ingredient.

Mrs. Phye stood with a hand on a hip and glared into those appraising eyes. Peter knew, and she knew he knew, and it only made it all the more infuriating to her. Peter could only wonder why as he shrunk away. Her sudden appearance was quite a shock to him, causing his heart to race and his stomach to feel queasy. There were several uncomfortable seconds of brow-beating, then she brushed past him to the pantry and pulled out bread and peanut butter. Peter slunk to the table and waited while she spread the peanut butter, shredding the bread to messy tatters in the process.

"Mom," he asked in the uncomfortable silence, "do you think there's anything living in our fridge?"

Dillon was waving his arms, shaking his head and mouthing the words, *NO, NO!*

Mrs. Phye stopped. "Is that funny?"

"Oh, no," said Peter, immediately sorry for even hoping to start a conversation with her. "I think someone was just pullin' my leg, that's all."

Mrs. Phye turned and breathed several heavy breaths with her back to him, looking down at the plate the sandwich was on. "Someone, huh? Why don't you take your sarcastic little remarks outside?" She turned and shoved the sandwich at him. "Go on, get out!" She spun him around and pushed him toward the door. Peter stumbled and knocked the door open, dropping his sandwich down the front of himself and onto the porch. Dillon was ejected from his shoulder and landed on the table.

"There you go, and now I have bugs in my house!"

And as if bugs were the worst thing in her house, Mrs. Phye slapped at Dillon with a rolled newspaper, causing the dirty dishes on the table to dance and clatter in a way to remind one they were brittle. Dillon fluttered about, from here to there, avoiding her and eventually landing high up on the cupboards. Mrs. Phye swiped madly, focused inexplicably on this single little bug, but couldn't reach him, her face red and shining, fly-away hair sticking to her sweaty forehead.

Peter hurried back in. "What'd I do, mom? ...Please don't hurt him!"

Things were banging and things were clanging, and Dillon flew out as soon as the door opened again. Mrs. Phye met Peter with another hard shove, sending him stumbling down the steps and sprawling into the yard.

The door slammed shut behind him.

Chapter Twenty-five
A Place Way Up There

The air outside held Peter's clothing against his skin like a wet blanket. He lay, hidden from view, in the tall meadow grass along with Dillon, looking up. There was no breeze to cut the thickness of the day. Tears trickled down Peter's cheek and pooled at the base of his throat. He wiped his eyes with the back of his hand, then dabbed his face with his shirt.

The clouds were plump and white, and gray along their undersides, which were flat, as though they lay upon a dome in the sky. They were stacked, mountains atop mountains, the sky around them pale blue and distant. Peter smiled. The billowy clouds looked solid enough for him to stand on. He wondered how high they actually went. He wondered how it might feel to stand atop them and look down.

Problems must surely seem small from there, he thought.

"I wonder what it's like, way up there," Dillon said, echoing Peter's thoughts.

Peter was suddenly aware of a certain depth to their friendship. Dillon hadn't mentioned the incident with his mother, which was, by Peter's estimate, most generous. Dillon's hands were clasped behind his head, and he and Peter looked up dreamily, Dillon, from where he lay atop the white flowered cap of a Queen Anne's lace, above Peter.

"My dad said he went above them once," answered Peter.

Dillon laughed.

"No, I mean it," said Peter.

"That's not possible for a living creature to do," said Dillon. "Even the birds say so."

Peter rolled his head to look at Dillon.

"Well, my father wouldn't lie," he said. "He said he would take me there in an airplane at the end of the summer, when we go to my uncle's house in Mississippi."

"Miss-iss-ip-eee. Now there's a mouthful," said Dillon, continuing to mull the word silently in his mouth like he was chewing taffy. "You sure you don't mean Muzz-sippy?"

"I know bigger words," Peter said. "Fort Michilimackinac."

"Fort Mich-la-*what*?"

"Or how about supercalifragilisticexpialidocious."

"You made that one up."

"No, it's real, I swear, from a song."

"Oh, well," Dillon said, "a song." He rolled his eyes. "Guess that lends it all the credibility it deserves."

The two were silent.

"You believe me, don't you?" asked Peter.

Dillon remained silent.

"About the clouds, I mean," Peter said.

"I know what y' mean," Dillon said, continuing to look up as he thought for a second or two. "Sure I do," he said. "Everything's possible."

He sounded lazy and unconvincing. Peter rolled his head again to watch the clouds.

"You know," said Dillon, "the horses tell me you'll go up there one day, 'cause you're a boy. Horses are special, just like boys. Hardly a single one comes or goes in this world without notice. The horses tell me that when a human loves 'em, they'll take 'em along, into the clouds when they die."

Dillon's eyes turned down and he lost his dreamy tone. "I'm just part of a brood," he said, "a swarm. I live one summer, and when it's over..." He looked down at Peter. "Whoever put me here was very thoughtless, indeed."

The two were silent again.

"Where do you go when... the summer ends?" asked Peter.

Dillon looked up again to avoid looking at Peter. "Oblivion."

"Oblivion?"

"The Forgotten," said Dillon. "For me... *For us*, it's the only way outta Efemera."

"And where is that?"

"Not sure. ...It's a place that eventually finds us and swallows us up. Where we grope endlessly in darkness, lookin' for things we've never even noticed we lost and can never hope t' find."

Dillon sounded as distant as the azure sky. Peter was touched for the first time by things once unimaginable. "I don't like the sound of that," he said.

"No, it sounds lonely," said Dillon, lazily again, but this time with a note of tired resignation. It seemed unfair to Peter, and it struck him how awful such a feeling must be, how awful it would be to live knowingly under such a burden. He felt suddenly immensely sorry for Dillon.

"What is The Forever?" he asked.

Dillon laughed. "A sublime bit of nonsense. Equally as absurd as Oblivion. No one ever gave it a thought till the birds put it in their heads. Now it's all they think about, and none a' those nitwits even knows how t' begin to imagine it!"

"Well how would you imagine it?"

"Wouldn't care t' try."

"Supposin' you did."

They were quiet while Peter waited.

"Alright," Dillon said. "Hmmmm... Alright... In that case... I'd imagine it to be... An endless, meaningful conversation among friends, where we play through the night into an endlessly recurring perfect summer day."

Wow! Now that was a thing Peter could understand. There was

quiet between them for a moment as a truck rattled slowly past in the distance. His imaginings had been bogged down by Cartesian coordinates and lines with arrows on both ends, and vectors with a point on one end and an arrow on the other; and the number *pi*, if anyone could even call that tireless tramp a number. Thinking big always caused Peter to think in mathematical terms, which he knew was no good. Math could be a downright fraud in philosophical applications. It was leading him, in his aforementioned efforts to reconcile certain occurrences and ideas, to begin to think of himself as lacking in mental capacity. Not that he figured himself stupid because of it, since no one else really knew the answers either, but more along the lines of feeding too big a problem into his calculator and getting error as the answer. Neither he nor anyone else was in possession of the accoutrements necessary to formulate a complete understanding of a great many things, and those who claimed they did always seemed to have their answers come up as EEEEEEEEE, as a default to some other wooly abstraction that begged for just one more sensory organ to help give form to its untenable mass.

But there was no such thing in this world, and any reasonable twelve-year-old could tell you that.

"You know," Peter said, "I looked up magicadas on our computer, and it says you come back every thirteen years."

"They say certain magicadas live on and on, forever and ever, accordin' to lore," replied Dillon. "Some in the brood I came from were as old as old can be. T' think of poor ol' Paw Tithnus; our legends tell us he can't even walk no more. ...He's Greek, so I never met 'em." Dillon smiled suddenly. "But he still sits 'n plays, blind as can be, smilin' an' a stompin' his foot."

"Maybe you'll be like him."

Dillon looked wistfully at Peter. "Don't sound like much more'n a fairy's existence to me. Gypsies, leap-froggin' through time. Never more'n acquaintances with real folk. Anyway, it's just a myth, just somethin' t' make some of us feel better."

"Then someday I'll take you with me," replied Peter.

Dillon smiled as he looked again toward the clouds.

Chapter Twenty-six
A Place To Begin

A subtle breeze began to blow, causing the Queen Anne's lace to bob back and forth. Peter looked at Dillon, whose hands were still clasped behind his head as he lay atop the gently rocking weed shaft enjoying the breeze, a satisfied smile in place.

"Here's what I think," Peter said, sitting up. "Someone *kidnapped* the Maestro!"

"Why y' think that?" asked Dillon casually, his eyes closed.

"Because he was singing somewhere near my room the night he disappeared."

Dillon sat up alert and looked around, then lowered his voice.

"Who knows this besides you?" He looked around again. "And me now?"

"Nobody."

"You're *sure?*"

"Yes."

Dillon placed his hands behind his head again and sat back while he thought.

"...Is it possible he could've been killed by accident?" asked Peter, the worry most obvious in his voice. Dillon tilted his head to look at him.

"Why would you ask that?"

"...Don't know," said Peter. "...Or... maybe 'cause I was reaching around in my messy room and might've crushed him... accidentally, I mean. I'd never do such a thing on purpose, but..."

"Calm down, Peter. You didn't crush him. Nobody can kill him. The Queen put a spell on him t' keep him from gettin' killed."

Peter was silent for a few seconds as he allowed himself Dillon's consolation. "Well," he said, finally, "then why doesn't she just put him back where he belongs?"

"She can't."

"Why not?"

"'Cause she's only Queen Of The Night, under whose domain the Realm of Efemera technically exists via a complicated juxtaposition of Ethereal Law, which states..."

Dillon paused.

"Which is to say," he continued, reading Peter's confusion, "but a part a' The Everything. And she don't have the power t' directly influence things outside her realm, such as creatures who only visit Efemera. ...Like you."

"Me?"

"Yep."

"...But I thought I was the same as you, only I just began to notice... according to the Commodore, that is."

"No. No, y' got it wrong somehow," said Dillon. "You're just visitin'. Only thing we really have in common is dreams, in which we may meet from time to time. We... me and everyone else... all live here, although some don't like t' think so, it's true. Some believe they have 'sponsors', bein' the pets a' humans, think they'll go along with 'em t' The Forever one day. And the birds... 'Course, they're smug in their confidence *they'll* leave for The Forever singin' the hours all day long, each silly, misguided flock singin' its own particular song and waitin' for the hand a' Creation t' recognize it an' come down and sweep 'em away. *The Miracle of Never Mind*, what a bunch a' hooey! Nothin' but a way t' lull a soul t' sleep."

Dillon paused and looked around as he thought. "'Course, there are the things of lower intelligence... snakes and fish and such. Humph!" Dillon laughed. "The things in your mama's fridge! I don't know if they even dream." He looked up in wonder. "It's kinda complicated, but the bottom line is this: the Queen is powerless t' make you do anything. She only exists in Dreamland, which is far removed from our clunky ol' world, and y' can't have power where y' don't actually exist. She's more like a persistent thought."

"Sure she exists," Peter said. "I've met her."

"We've all met her," Dillon said, "way off in Dreamland."

Peter tried to imagine how that made a difference.

"But can't she bring on winter?" he asked.

"She can let it happen," Dillon said. "After all, what's winter really, but an absence of joy?"

An absence of joy? thought Peter. "It's not that bad," he said.

"Guess I wouldn't know," said Dillon. "But I do know it's the end a' many a lifetime."

But what was a lifetime? Whether one summer or a hundred, there would always be a last one, and Peter figured it would be hard to face whenever it came. Winter limited numbers, but it never once diminished summer's essence, and that's how he chose to view it. If winter was the doorway to Oblivion, then Oblivion was a void into which those lacking foresight inevitably fell. It could be crossed. You just had to find the way. Eat more and build a bigger house. Leave a trail of bread crumbs so others might find you. If only Dillon could know another springtime. And why not? If it was *imaginable*, wasn't it possible? Maybe he could keep him in his room, Peter was thinking, as a pet. They would set things right together and share winter dreams: candy canes and lights, and the vastness of the sky lain bare... and there was room in those dreams for a magicada, and all of Efemera, even in winter. Yes, Peter was certain, more than for Dillon's sake: something always comes next. He'd have to hide him, though.

"Now," Dillon continued, "since no one would be able t' kill the Maestro, and no primitive'd be smart enough t' plot to abduct him for any higher purpose... and, since those who live in Efemera tend to need music as much as anyone else, I suspect the guilty party t' be part of a criminal element *outside* Efemera."

"Kidnapped," said Peter.

"I'm inclined t' think so," said Dillon. "Someone not *quite* part of Efemera. Just didn't know they were so close t' the source. Dangerous business... more so'n you know. You'd be, after all, a prime suspect to anyone who gave it an ounce of thought. ...I think it might be prudent if we kept this under our hats for now. No need to involve Lucien and his hobgoblin sleuths." Dillon whispered as he leaned forward. "In fact, I think most of us... Hold on, who's that?"

"Dunno," said Peter.

A portly gray pigeon stared from a wire at the far edge of the meadow.

"How long's he been there?"

"Dunno."

"Hold on," said Dillon. "Hey! You there!"

The pigeon pointed to himself.

"Yeah, you. Can I help you?"

The pigeon flew off.

"*That's right, stoolie!*" shouted Dillon. "*Fly away, snoop!*"

"Who was that?" Peter asked.

"No worry. Just some sneak tryin' t' stick his beak where it don't belong. ...We were just talkin' 'bout the weather. We know the question that really needs answerin'," said Dillon as he leaned back again and clasped his hands behind his head, feeling himself the true depths of friendship. "And I say we begin by lookin' into the very bottom of the criminal element's cesspool. Tonight. ...Looks like rain, don't y' think?"

Chapter Twenty-seven
Finnegan's Awake

"Here Ki-tty, ki-tty, ki-tty."

Mrs. Phye called to the cats with her tongue thick again and manner unsteady as she put together another messy string of slurred words and incoherent sounds. Boog sat on the wood pile behind the house with Algernon and watched.

"Meoww-woww-woww-woww-oww... ha-ha-ha-*HA!*" Mrs. Phye meowed and laughed an unseemly laugh, red-faced and more belligerent than ever. She was in her nightgown, and spun round and round in wobbly circles before stumbling and crashing hard to the ground.

"She's nuts!" said Boog.

"More like three sheets to the wind," said Algernon. "Sheesh! You smell it?"

Boog sniffed then gave his head a quick shake. Mrs. Phye crouched with her hands on her knees. "Here, Ki-tty, ki-tty."

"What's she think she's doing?" asked Boog.

"Singing, I think."

"*That's* singing?"

Mrs. Phye stood up and tottered toward them, when the door at the back of the house suddenly burst open and Mr. Phye hurried out, hair askance and puffy eyes, high-stepping in his bare feet through the wet grass. The cats jumped down and ran off into the bushes.

"Lois!" he cried in an enraged whisper. "What-Are-You-Doing!? Get inside, right this instant!"

Mrs. Phye spun around and stumbled backward against the wood pile. "Oh, so handsome in his nightshirt!" she said, pushing forward and staggering toward Mr. Phye, throwing her arms out. "How 'bout a great big kiss!" she said, puckering her lips and closing her eyes like some love-struck carp. Mr. Phye caught her as she fell forward and held her upright.

"Good Lord woman! Have you been drinking *again*?"

"No. ...*No!* ...Just a lil' nip t' put me t' sleep," she said, followed by a couple of sloppy smacks of her lips.

"Put you to sleep is right! Come on," Mr. Phye looked around. "In we go." And he hurried Mrs. Phye through the back door.

Chapter Twenty-eight
In The Underworld

Rocco Colossimo was a burly raccoon, big even by raccoon standards. A nighttime prowler, Rocco slept all day in an underground lair within the barred confines of the shadowy graveyard. No one dared disturb surly, burly Rocco Colossimo during the day. He was a volatile mixture of business and pleasure; of violence and compassion; of light and darkness. Dawn was the safest time to approach him, when his carousing and nocturnal revelries were finished; when, softened and befuddled by excess, he was most likely in high spirits, or, at the very least, intoxicated into affability.

In short, Rocco was known to be a happy drunk. He liked to temper his excessively debauched evenings with the soporific lilt of musical religiosity; a concession to his conscience with what he considered the pleasanter aspect of religion, and he clung devotedly to that single facet (casually dismissing the rest) since it was to him, above all, enjoyable. He wasn't the least bit interested, you see, in letting his conscience become a slave to the broader aspects of the music's intent (a Siren's call, he liked to term it), so that his conscience might, in turn, turn around and try to make a slave of him. No, no, he was simply fond of listening to Matins, when the birds began to sing in the gray first light, always with joyous, sentimental tears in his eyes; then, to retire and begin anew his immoral habits, late next day.

And so it was as Peter and Dillon approached.

It was well past midnight, that formidable and arbitrary barrier Peter had tried unsuccessfully to breach several times in his life, when they'd started for the cemetery. Peter was, for that matter, a very hard sleeper, causing Dillon to work for nearly thirty minutes to wake him with unheeded beckonings in his ear. The time was so late -- or so early -- that the numbers indicated by the hands on the kitchen clock seemed completely absurd to Peter. Never having met the darker side of four o'clock before, it was, he quickly decided, an ugly step-child, one that nobody cared to visit. Or, more appropriately, a ghost, mostly because the stillness and darkness and shadows were more conducive to ghosts and ghostly forebodings, but also because of a vague notion he'd had about time's inherent nature, made more clear by the circumstances. And that was the thing: Peter had always considered sleep time, the time that exists during sleep, to be as meaningless and inconsequential as that of dream time, and that made it spectral in at least one possible sense, living a life of its own in the æther of unconsciousness. And it was naturally alarming for Peter to find that a world might actually exist outside his former awareness, a world which was bigger than him, saying that it would go on with or without him. Peter found a certain thought pertaining to time nearly unbearable: supposing that daytime wasn't so different from sleep time, and that his whole life was inconsequential? He was suddenly staring right into the face of something he'd been blissfully unaware of all along, something huge that normally passed through him almost as easily as cosmic radiation. And it frightened him.

That is, when he wasn't thinking about "real" ghosts and ghostly forebodings.

And so it was that four o'clock in the morning became to Peter the closest thing to a ghost he'd ever met. ...Or might ever meet, he hoped as he looked warily about. The last thing he wanted was to run into Pops Barnsworth's ghost out there! Together, he and Dillon made their way in darkness along the old dirt road, Peter scratching absently at the giant, indurated lump of a mosquito bite on his forearm and feeling a certain otherworldliness in walking with such a familiar hour's ghost. It was as though he'd left his body and walked outside himself. Nighttime had transfigured the entire route, so familiar by light of day, so that the trees hung lower over the road. The air was even different, filled with coolness and wetness; and the lack of any other sound made his scuffling along sound loud, which he noticed, so picked up his feet. But when he did that, he stumbled too frequently, in potholes and on stones, and so had mostly been looking down, peering at the road as if into a stream he was wading through, misgauging its surface in exactly the same way. When he finally decided to look up, there, just ahead, was a parting in the trees.

The graveyard.

Peter was glad to have Dillon with him. They made their way through the wrought iron bars of the hamlet's most joyless place and crept between ashen tombstones, across dewy wet grass. There was a star, bright as an approaching airplane; and clouds, illuminated by what remained of a big full corn moon, ran along the sky, the wind pushing them and rattling the trees, some of which creaked as if something very heavy swung from their boughs.

What a disquieting thought.

"I don't like this," Dillon said to Peter.

Peter stood among the pallid gravestones, fearful himself, and swallowed hard. "It's the same place it is in the daylight," he said.

Hoot! Hoot-Hoot!

An owl hooted three times, and Dillon hopped from Peter's shoulder to the top of his head. There was a rustle from somewhere in the darkness. Peter held his breath. Things moved... And then... They didn't. The wind blew. There was the rasp of branches rubbing together, which sounded like someone crying. Peter stared hard into the shadows. Then, from behind a chipped and tilted headstone...

An enormous raccoon emerged, swaggering drunkenly, along with three punchy, tough-talking toadies.

"...So when the captains are too strong and the don weak, the result is insubordination. And when the don's too strong and the captains weak, the result's a total mess," waxed Rocco philosophically, if not a little incoherently, mingling declarative with interrogative sentences the way he tended to do at high ebb. "Y' can't sacrifice balance for execution, or vice versa, know what I mean? Y' can't have captains and dons with unequal abilities, know what I'm sayin'?"

Peter heard the quiet *plop, plop, plops* as the toadies hopped along behind him.

"Hey Rocco," one croaked, "we got company."

Peter stood as Rocco and his minions approached.

"Careful with these guys," Dillon whispered.

Peter nodded.

"I'm Peter Phye," Peter said bravely. "And this is Dillon Hopper, from the Deep South." Peter pointed to the top of his head.

Rocco didn't say anything as he waddled toward them with his head lowered, black eyes shining through his black mask in the moonlight. Discontinuously, the toadies followed... first this one, then that one, then that...

Rocco stopped.

"I know who ya are. I know *everything* that goes on around here. Ya took one in the back from that sicko 'cross the meadow. I saw the whole thing. Poor cub, what were ya thinkin'? Ya gotta tackle those kinda problems head-on."

"Yeah, we seen everything!" chimed a bellicose little toady.

"Question is," Rocco growled, "whatta ya want?"

"We want..."

A tree creaked loudly. Peter looked up. The toadies hopped ahead of Rocco and stopped at Peter's feet. One squatted and cracked the knuckles of his fist.

"We want," Peter continued, looking down, "some information."

"Information!" cried Rocco. He glanced at his toadies with a hearty laugh.

The toadies all laughed.

"Knowledge!" shouted Rocco, laughing harder and harder until he broke into a violent, hacking cough, nearly causing himself to be sick.

The toadies all looked at one another and smirked.

"That all?" Rocco asked after a minute or so, gasping and wheezing as he worked to regain himself.

"The Maestro's missing," said Peter.

"That a fact?" smiled Rocco, wiping his eyes.

The toadies exchanged nods and smug looks.

"He's missing, and the Queen of the Night is very upset."

Rocco hesitated. The toadies stopped with their smirking and smug looks.

Silence.

"Go away," Rocco said, completely sober. "We don't need the Queen nosin' around."

"Yeah, go away!" said one of his toadies.

"No," said Peter. "Not 'till you help us."

The toadies all gasped and looked at one another, then rose to their haunches.

"Easy boys," Rocco said. Then, to Peter, "Who says I know anything?"

"You did. You just said you know everything. Didn't he, Dillon?"

There was a dumb silence.

"Well, Peter..." Dillon hesitated. "Ah, Mr. Colossimo may have been speakin' rhetorically. Uh, I mean, I'd hate to call anyone anything but honest, leastwise till I know..."

"Shut up, grasshopper!" A toady hopped onto Peter's shoe and curled his sock into his fist. "How 'bout I make an example a' this one."

"Yeah," said one of the others. "No one gets cute with Rocco!"

And they all hopped toward Peter.

"No," said Rocco.

The toadies stopped.

"Come with me," said Rocco to Peter, turning and walking away, "minus the grasshopper."

"Ah... magicada," chirped Dillon. "Ah... Mr. Colossimo, grasshoppers are dirty and uncouth, and I don't chew or spit."

"Shut up, grasshopper! Who cares!" A toady was pointing at him. "Now get down here! *Now!*"

Peter looked at Rocco, who stopped and turned.

"He will be all right, won't he?" Peter asked.

"Keep an eye on him boys, 'till I get back. And mind yer manners," said Rocco.

Dillon hopped from Peter's head to a tombstone and fidgeted while the toadies squatted below and rubbed their fists. Peter and Rocco walked out of earshot.

"Look kid, I don't need no heat from the Queen. Don't wan' her gettin' heavy and bringin' winter down on us early, know what I mean? That wouldn't be no good for no one. Now I'm not one t' mess with another guy's racket, understand? Everyone's entitled t' make a livin' the best way they know how. I'm runnin' a pretty smooth operation, see, between trash cans and the gardens, and the trinket trade, an' I don't want no bugs messin' me up, know what I mean? Or cat or bird... or the-man-in-moon, for that matter."

Rocco paused and breathed heavily as he stopped to look at Peter, his gaze softening. "The enemy of my enemy is my friend, know what I'm sayin'? Look at your friend over there, he knows what I mean. Just point the bees in the right direction, that's what I'm sayin'. Are ya hearin' me? Sometimes ya can't tackle a problem all by yourself, but'cha can still tackle it head-on. No crime in employin' someone with mutual interests t' do yer dirty work. Keeps yer hands clean, know what I mean? Keeps others wonderin' who actually pulls the trigger, an' that ain't all bad."

He looked at Peter.

"Are you saying I should work for you, or that *you* should work for me?" Peter asked.

Rocco smiled.

"Neither and both. This world can be pretty and this world can be rough. There's only one way out for guys like me, and it ain't pretty: grimacin', legs stickin' straight in the air. T' see it first-hand kinda shatters the myth of peaceful slumber, if ya know what I mean? (Peter nodded) I gotta take it where I can get it, know what I'm sayin'?" Rocco laughed. "Ain't no guarantees for me. ...But you're different," he added, more soberly again, almost friendly. "Better'n me. ...I been thinkin', all a' these stiffs buried here mighta got it right," he said. "Etch your name in stone." Rocco slapped the grave-stone he was standing alongside and nodded knowingly at Peter. "Put my boys t' work on it today." He pointed down toward its base. Though hard to see, there was the beginning of a rudimentary little R scratched onto the stone at about the height of a toady, visible due likely entirely to the propitious full moon reflecting off it at the proper angle at that particular time of year... that and the toadies were keeping the grass cropped short all around the base. "Hard work," announced Rocco, "but that'll be there till the end a' time."

"Or for at least as long as the stone lasts," answered Peter.

Incredulous, Rocco stared him down.

"This whole world ain't nothin' but one big rock," said Rocco, "with us growin' on it, see? Nothin' outlasts a rock. And that's the end a' my free advice, understand?"

Peter nodded. "I think so," he said, but wondering what had been meant by "trinket trade." Then, thinking suddenly of things missing from his own back yard: "Have you seen my Major John Grande?"

"Your what?"

"Major John Grande. He's a guy with a shiny space suit and helmet. He talks when you pull the string on his back, says..."

"What would I want with a Major John Grande?" spat Rocco. "Believe me kid, there's no market for used goofy action figures. But I ask you, what's in all this for me?"

"For you?" asked Peter.

"Yeah, nothin's free, kid. I help you, you help me. Didn't cha get it?"

Peter stared.

"So... whatta ya got... t' trade... for... my knowledge?" Rocco spelled it out for Peter, who simply rolled his eyes upward and twisted his mouth.

"I can't think of anything," he said. "'Cept toys."

"No, I already told ya," said Rocco slowly, "there's no market for your crappy toys. I stumble over a toy every time I turn around. Nothin' depreciates faster'n a toy."

Peter stared for a second then shrugged.

"Ya come all the way out here in the middle a' the night, and got nothin'?"

"Ah, it's actually morning. Very early morning," said Peter. "Just a head start on the day."

Silence. Then...

"See ya later, kid." Rocco turned to leave.

"*Wait!*" said Peter. "Whatta y' want?"

Rocco stopped.

"Hmm," he said. "Now yer talkin. Ya live on the other side a' the trees, right? Jus' south a' here?"

"Ahhh..." (Navigating by ded-reckoning was always tricky for Peter) "...Yes," he said, turning to point. "Back there."

"Yeah. Well, tell ya what, I'll be around," said Rocco. He looked at Peter for a second, breathing loudly through his nose. "I suggest..." (Two more heavy breaths) "...Ya ask the birds where the Maestro is." He smiled and nodded his head with a wink, as if he believed he had lain it all very nicely in Peter's lap.

"The birds?" asked Peter.

"Yeah, tweet-tweet."

Rocco laughed, then turned and swaggered back toward where the others were waiting. Peter watched until he disappeared into the shadows, then looked to the trees, which creaked again. White eyes shone from above, then vanished.

"Let's go in and get cleaned up boys!" he heard Rocco cry exuberantly. "Almost time for Matins! Oh, how I love the sound a' those little birdies, gets me right here, every time. Makes me feel I'm bound for The Forever on the flutterin' wings of fairies. Makes me glad t' be alive!"

Dillon flew to Peter's shoulder. A rooster crowed from way over at Mrs. Barrow's house. The toadies all laughed. And then came the twitter of the day's first real bird.

Chapter Twenty-nine
A Bugaboo

"There he goes," said Dillon.

Peter was walking back toward his house, along the dirt road with Dillon on his shoulder. Dillon had been giving his opinions on their most recent encounter, saying things like Rocco should eat less red meat and exercise more, and that he had a bad way of phrasing everything as a question, causing one to "waggle their head incessantly" while they listened to him. Peter said he figured that was his way of making sure whoever he was talking to stayed involved in the conversation, and Dillon had said he might be right "'cause he sure seemed t' like t' talk." Then he said -- and Peter had to quietly comb his recollection for this part -- he had grown tired of the insults toward the both of them, which was why he'd had to step up. He said he was only "an inch away from thrashin' those mouthy little toadies" when he broke off and noted a certain someone going somewhere.

"There *who* goes?" asked Peter.

They were walking up the driveway by that time, toward the back of the house. Peter saw the yard and the wood pile, but only faintly in moonlight, being still very dark outside otherwise.

"A bugaboo," Dillon said. "Right over there."

He pointed. Peter looked but saw nothing except a small crop of toadstools growing alongside the wood pile, barely distinguishable except for the way the moonlight reflected off them.

"Toadstools?"

"Just watch," Dillon said.

Peter watched, and one stood up and scampered off toward the house, then stopped halfway to squat and resemble a toadstool again. Then, a few seconds later, up it jumped and ran to the porch, straight to the back door, lifted the screen from the bottom corner, and disappeared into the house.

"Ew! What's a bugaboo?"

"Usually trouble," Dillon said. "Come on, I'll show ya." He flew off toward the house.

Peter hurried to the porch, where Dillon motioned for him to open the screen door, indicating silence with a finger to his lips. Peter pulled the creaky door open as quietly as possible, and Dillon fluttered to his shoulder.

"Over there," he whispered in Peter's ear. "Down the steps."

"In the basement?" asked Peter.

"*Shh.* Go on."

"What the heck's a bugaboo?" demanded Peter, preparing to assess the ratio of benefit to risk. To be sure, profit in this instance might be only of the narrowest margins, depending on the value of a bugaboo, since Peter was officially barred from the basement: mom's orders. Not to say there hadn't been one or two secret forays into it while she was napping, hasty little incursions which had Peter chicken-walking about on tip-toes, probing the cluttered darkness with trusty Grande Expedition Marauder's Penlight held out in front of him like a white cane, way too freaked out to thoroughly investigate the things he spied in its beam, afraid to incriminate himself by disturbing the least speck of dust, starting and cowering at every little sound like a nervous cat. No matter though, since things seemed clear enough above ground, if not below. Clear as they needed to be. Bugaboo or not, the basement was a dank and gloomy transformation chamber, no place for a child, all full of dark magic and darker elixirs; people were stewed and soused down there, and returned to the daylight shambling zombies until the Queen Of The Night could change them back... and then they were drawn inescapably back, again and again, mind switched on, mind switched off, flying uncontrollably between airy bliss and the depths of woe. And, while in this perpetual state of metamorphosis, no one, not even the person, could ever say whether they were here or there, leaving everyone to deal with the fact that they were really neither.

But they could still be mean. A graveyard after midnight was one thing, but few things inspired more fear in Peter than going against his mother. By golly, the last thing he wanted was to be caught coming out that door!

So it was with much trepidation that he tip-toed down the tiled steps.

"That's it," Dillon said as they stopped at the bottom.

It was pitch black.

"Turn the light on," said Dillon in a whisper.

Peter flipped the switch...

...And a tiny little man blinked from where he sat on a table-top with a giant bottle stuck in his mouth. "*Hey!*" he exclaimed, fumbling to set it down and watching Peter as he pushed a cork back into the top. He wore a domed brown hat that looked like the top of one of the toadstools outside, and might still have easily been confused for one, had it not been for the bottle, more than three times his size. He crept slowly behind it.

"You see?" Dillon said in a normal voice. "A bugaboo. Must belong t' someone in the house." And then, accounting for the bottles: "*Whoa-ho-ho!* Single malt!" He cleared his throat, and then proceeded delicately, "Does someone in your house have a drinkin' problem?"

"No," said Peter.

"Then why so much..."

"I don't know."

Dillon studied Peter for a second or two, who remained impassive. "Well," Dillon said at last, "that's *someone's* bugaboo there, and whoever's it is, they're lettin' 'em run amok." He leaned close and whispered, "He's not sure y' really see him. He's watching you through that bottle. See? Walk on up to him and snatch his hat. If y' steal his hat and plant it in the ground, he'll be your slave."

"Really?"

"Yep. Just see that y' keep tendin' to it."

"But you said that about Chance, too."

"What?"

"That I could make him my slave if I captured him. Remember?"

"No, I said he'd grant y' wishes, but then... Never mind! I'm right about this!"

Peter debated with himself. "But what if he's not our bugaboo?" he whispered.

"Don't matter. You'll be doin' someone a favor."

Peter took a deep, nervous breath.

"Do they bite?"

"Don't think so," said Dillon. "Looks like he's got no teeth anyway."

Peter moved toward the bottle. The bugaboo stayed crouched where he was, his clever, toothless little grin fading as he watched. Peter, more than a little anxious himself, looked at Dillon, who motioned for him to go ahead. Peter crept closer. The bugaboo stood still, peering through the bottle, over the brown liquid inside. Peter snatched him by the back of his brown jacket, wiggling and thrashing as he dangled from his thumb and forefinger, no bigger than a small potato, and proportioned like one, as well, with spindly little arms and legs.

"Go on, Peter, take his hat and toss him outside!" said Dillon excitedly.

"I don't wanna be mean to him."

"Mean to him? He's vermin! Look at him, stealin' whisky." Dillon looked around. "And by the looks of it, he's messin' your house up, too. Keep him around and he'll loosen the knobs and hinges on your cupboards... or worse yet, steal your whisky!" he said, sneering into the bugaboo's face.

"But he's cute," said Peter, cocking his head to examine the creature. "And I thought you were gonna quit bein' so judgmental?"

The bugaboo nodded enthusiastically. "I was just dustin' the bottles," he said with a lisp and a brogue that reminded Peter of a leprechaun's.

"Oh look, he talks," said Peter, holding him more tightly by his jacket as he continued to squirm.

"'Just doostin' the bottles,'" said Dillon, mocking his brogue. "From the inside?"

"Aw, I was just sloshin' the pretty liquids, that's all, makin' sure t'was clean all round."

"Sloshin' it around is right," said Dillon. "We saw what you were doin'! ...Take his hat and toss him out Peter."

"Don't toss me out!" the bugaboo implored of Peter. "Please, t'isn't safe anymore. Tis driven me to drink, it has, an' I beg your forgiveness." He reached up and removed his hat, clutching it securely against his chest, revealing a bald, wrinkly pate.

"Are you sure we need to be so drastic, Dillon?" asked Peter. "You said bugaboo's are *usually* trouble, remember?"

"Um-um-um, ain't you the one. Mr. Memory. Sure do have a fine recollection for the things everyone says all a sudden. 'Course, can't say it's been all that convenient t' me tonight. ...Jus' take his hat or you'll be sorry!"

"You know, you're only lucky no one notices you stealin'," said Peter, turning to admonish the bugaboo, who cast his eyes downward with a chastened frown, shaking his head slowly in a show of remorse.

"Aye, an' lucky we all are, indeed," he said. "For I never take more'n a wee doonk... just enough t' sharpen m' wit. Tis a cruel world out there, full a' thugs an' cut-throats, and it's not been the same since that fool stole the cricket away."

Peter shot Dillon a glance. "What fool?"

The bugaboo smiled slyly.

"Put me down and I'll tell ya."

"Never mind," said Dillon. "*You're* the only fool around here. Toss him out, Peter. And keep his hat."

"Aye, but I know of a bigger fool. ...One with *fur*," the bugaboo whispered to Peter.

119

Peter set him on the table. "Who?" he asked.

The bugaboo calmly straightened his jacket, then, with a shifty smile, looked down at the backs of his outstretched hands.

"Don't Peter! Take his hat first!"

The bugaboo hopped to the floor, spry as could be, and ran for the steps. "I'll take me chances outside!" he yelled as he pulled his hat back over his head and scampered around the corner, out of sight. There was a light-footed patter of feet on the steps.

And he was gone.

Chapter Thirty
Into The Rabbit's Hole

Technically (in his own mind anyway) Peter hadn't broken any rules by slipping out early in the morning, as opposed to leaving in the middle of the night, a point he preferred not to defend if at all possible. For, being conceptually rational, he hadn't bothered to ask his parents for permission. It had been a spur of the moment decision really; an idea of Dillon's, and a fruitful one at that. But the fruit of their labor was nothing more than a mixed message, implying fur on the one hand, and feathers on the other. And a cricket? The entire growing season depended on a single cricket?

"Why sure," Dillon had said. "I thought everybody knew the Maestro was a cricket."

Peter would never have imagined it. And he still couldn't imagine why anyone would want to disrupt the music. And, as Dillon had said, who could trust a bugaboo? Of course, Rocco Colossimo was obviously no choir boy, despite his love for singing birds. But he seemed an honorable crook, and Peter kind of liked him.

He would need to sort things out later with Dillon. He lay in his bed, relieved that that part was over, and fell instantly asleep.

The chirp of a pious bird woke him later... it thought The Creator was listening. There had been no dreams, only a perceptible lapse in time since his last thought. Too hot and too bright to sleep any longer, and though still tired, Peter opened his eyes and was surprised not to find Dillon waiting for him. He rose and pulled yesterday's shorts back on again, troubled by Dillon's absence.

The Commodore, along with Lucien, was waiting when Peter arrived in the woods late that morning. They were talking to one-another as he approached. Then they stopped and both looked at him.

"Peter," the Commodore said, "Mr. Lucien was wondering if he might have a word with you."

Peter hesitated as the Commodore stood before him, a reassuring smile in place.

"This isn't a very good time," Peter replied, feeling Lucien study his response.

The Commodore began again, "Well, I'm sorry to..."

"Not good?" interrupted Lucien. He stepped forward on the branch where he was, his wings tucked behind his back.

"No," said Peter. "I'm looking for my friend, Dillon Hopper."

Lucien smiled. "We're talking to him now," he said, his smile turning frigid. "Please, follow me." And he extended a wing.

"Probus, I trust this will be a friendly talk. He is, after all, our guest," said the Commodore with surprising assertiveness. He watched Lucien with his chin down in a measured silence. Peter waited. Lucien's frigid smile gradually gave way.

"Certainly," he replied. "Friendly. ...*This* time, anyway. We're always friendly to those who *cooperate*." The corner of his mouth twitched as he glanced down at Peter.

Peter followed him into the woods. The dusky owl flew from one tree limb to the next, staying always just ahead of Peter. And all the animals along the way watched as they passed. They stopped Peter when they could to quickly introduce themselves. They smiled and shook his hand, leaving Peter unsure as to whether he was being greeted by them as a celebrity or a criminal. He thought of his friend, Roland Plessinger, the time he was taken out of the classroom by the teacher to be paddled. Peter, never having personally suffered the indignity, could only imagine what went on out there in the hallway, pieced together from the first and second-hand exaggerations. Roland, it had been said, normally took his floggings bent over with a proud, defiant, straight face -- emotionless, unflinching -- while the teacher whaled away in a fury trying to elicit some response -- she couldn't be satisfied until there was *some* response. And, when it was clear he would deny her that, Roland said she resorted to choking him, he, maintaining his noble indifference all the while... although tears, as a natural result of this, did occasionally form in the corners of his eyes, as they would for anyone being choked. That was a law of physics. There was even a fellow student able to "collaborate" at least one instance of this, a pesky little braggart who'd apparently been skipping school that day to hook-up with older girls from the junior high. He claimed to have happened to look in through a window just in time – well, not so much a window as a hole in the roof, since that's where he was at the time, stealing lost kick-balls and finding a Rolex watch, which he gave to his dad -- and he added the part where the teacher hit Roland repeatedly over the head with a trash can, which Roland suddenly remembered as well, although rather dismissively. In fact, the boy went on and on until even Roland couldn't stand it anymore and chased him away for exaggerating and jeopardizing his credibility. (He was thinking about a lawsuit, you see.) And so, with so many distractions, all Peter could know for sure was that the teacher took her sturdy wood paddle with her, which hung, just like a boat oar, near the door of the classroom as a gentle reminder.

Peter drifted in his tired haze as he followed Lucien, recalling he and the other children, hushed to an expectant silence, looking at one-another, waiting. There was the teacher talking. And someone else... Mr. Moody, the principal most likely...

Pop! ...Pop! ...Pop!

And there it was! And then the giggles from the others in the classroom! Roland had thrown snowballs on the playground. (Some, theoretically, might have had rocks in their centers.) All the children had giggled until the door opened and the teacher walked back in, followed by a red-faced, tearful Roland Plessinger...

"Hello there, Peter Phye! I'm Artie Burrow, and this is my wife, Beatrice!" said an enthusiastic, elderly mole, jarring Peter from his daydream as he passed. They just wanted him to know that. It was becoming clear to Peter that some had taken to hedging their bets, especially now that Lucien had shown such interest in him, figuring that if anything bad should happen they could be among his last thoughts. ...Well, who could know for sure? There were always the stories about horses and house pets.

Peter followed Lucien to the furthest reaches of Efemera, to the places where things became dark and hazy and refused to coalesce. The trees grew bigger there and blocked out much of the light from above. Glowing eyes watched from the shadows, winking in and out of discernible existence. Peter saw an old tree in the murky distance, a tree he vaguely recognized. It had always loomed in the darkness like a giant monster ready to devour stragglers and wayfarers. Peter had seen it before, through the dark forest, but always at a distance, too scared to approach, too scared to venture far enough from the beaten path. Lucien led Peter toward it.

There was a hole at its base that led underground. Peter looked up as he entered, as the tree spread its limbs and swallowed him up. The hole was very large, like that of some tremendous rabbit burrow, and once inside, dysphoria took hold of him. The dirt walls were unpleasantly cool and damp, the air humid and filled with the strong seminal smell of worms; and Peter imagined suddenly losing himself in a demented Wonderland, all full of every manner of nonsense and foolishness, like that caterpillar Alice met -- smoking -- and the mushroom he told her to eat... and the fact that she ate it and other things when she shouldn't have! The nearest thing Peter could think of to that sort of impulsiveness was his one-year-old cousin, Roger, who lived in Luna Pier, and who was always causing Peter to regret handing him things because he just ended up lunging to fetch them right back from his mouth every time. Shoving things in his mouth was all the kid knew how to do. Peter would agree: those Alice stories were certainly good for stirring the imagination, veering off in any direction the way they did without confinement of reason, but listening to her get away with them sure set a bad precedent! He didn't care for them. No sir. He never said so, though. His mother used to read them to him -- and he liked that – but he had to act like he was falling asleep so as not to have to hear too much, and hoped that what he did hear didn't disturb his sleep... and, like it or not, even though they were considered time-honored and proper bedtime stories, that was how he felt.

But now he feared his own thinking had verged on that of Alice's, just like the dreams she had often caused him. He and Lucien plodded their way beneath ground with heavy, downward steps on a firmly packed earthen floor, those aforementioned feelings of wild unease – feelings he might later equate with suffocating claustrophobia -- working steadily to undo him. Light from the entrance was blocked by Peter's snug approximation to the walls, and he moved along, guided by this same approximation, until his eyes grew accustomed to the dark. A duller glow from the far end of the cramped tunnel emerged then to guide their way, and with no way to turn about and go back, Peter felt the thorough breadth of his entanglement. Ancillary passages opened here and there as the two worked their way ever deeper, some carrying sparse light of their own, and others, utterly black and forbidding. Peter heard angry, muffled shouting from down one of them as he passed.

"...You want this? Huh? *Huh?* I'll do it, I swear! Then tell me! *Tell me!*"

...As well as a shameful bit of pleading and whimpering. His heart raced as he crouched and duck-walked with his shoulders barely clearing the sides. He followed Lucien until, after awhile, they reached an open room to their left.

Peter was told to sit.

It was humid in there, and terribly stuffy, with a dim light shining on him through a single hole in the dirt ceiling that opened like a chimney vent to somewhere far above. Peter's breath, which came in labored pants from his open mouth, stuck to his face in wet droplets. The solitary light shone in his eyes when he looked up. He sat on a rickety wooden chair that creaked as he shifted nervously, first with arms folded, then while sitting on his hands, then, again, arms folded uncomfortably on his chest. There was a muffled silence as Lucien stood with his back to him. He turned slowly. Peter saw nothing of him, save a shining beak and flashing eyes.

"So," he began, his voice monotone and mechanical within the dampened acoustics of the room, "what did you and one Rocco Colossimo have to say to one another in the wee hours of the morning?"

Peter wondered how he knew. The air circulation in the room was seemingly nonexistent, and he breathed and re-breathed his own stale breath, which caused his heart to pound. He was certain Lucien could hear it.

"Rocco Colossimo?" he asked, as calmly as he was able.

"Rocco Colossimo. Raccoon, a.k.a., Mr. Scrillion, R. Coco, Mr. Big, and the Big R. ...Brigand, loan-shark, extortionist. ...*Libertine*," replied Lucien with a slow sneer, gazing at Peter all the while, shining eyes fixed and unblinking.

"Nothing," replied Peter, shaking his head with nary a hesitation.

But he was always a bad liar.

Lucien stepped forward into the light, making himself suddenly seem to appear. "Really," he said. "You left your house without your parents' permission. ...Let's see..." He pulled a note pad from under his wing. "One, Lois Phye, housewife of dubious skill, age forty, former magazine editor, consuming love of spirits... (Spirits? wondered Peter) ...And one, Arthur Phye, of the county road commission, age forty-five, *work*-aholic." Lucien stopped short. "You say you left their home, in the middle of the night, without permission, to visit a raccoon, a known underworld figure, in a graveyard before dawn. ...All for 'nothing?'"

Peter held a finger up. "Actually, it was very early in the morning, not the middle of the night."

Lucien stared coldly. "Is it also true," he continued, "that the Maestro was last heard orchestrating from your bedroom, within their house?"

Warmth seared Peter's face and neck. "I wouldn't say that was a certainty," he said, feeling his heart surge again.

Lucien's pupils widened, and he smiled. "Ah, but *we* can."

Peter was suddenly prepared to say just about anything he

thought Lucien might want to hear! He was tired of being involved. He was appalled at his own weakness! And though he really knew nothing at all, in his fright, the names of every animal in Efemera came rushing to his head, foremost of which being those of Artie and Beatrice Burrow.

But he controlled himself.

Lucien sensed his fear and stepped backward from the light, transfiguring himself again into something exaggerated by shadows.

"So now, tell me, Peter, what did Mr. Colossimo have to say?"

His voice was gentler.

"Nothing. Really," said Peter. "He told me to ask the birds."

"The birds?"

"Yeah. That's all. Ask the birds."

"Did he say which birds?"

"No. I promise."

"So strange, for him to implicate the birds, don't you think? So pious. So devoted to singing the hours. They go straight to The Forever when they leave Efemera. ...Or so it's said."

Peter could see Lucien was smiling.

"I'm a bird. (Peter suddenly realized that.) I know several cardinals personally, and they would be shocked by the implication." Lucien turned away from Peter. Then, spun his head around -- and only his head! -- then blinked. "Are you *sure* you're telling me the truth?" he asked harshly. "You know, we have ways of finding out. ...Severe ways! ...Unpleasant ways!"

"I am. I know. I don't know. Really, you've gotta believe me." Peter was terrified. "Please, may I go now?"

Lucien turned his body to correctly align it with his head.

"You may," he said, composed once again. "...For now."

Peter stood up and ducked through the doorway, brushing the ceiling with his head on the way out. He heard the *whish* of a spray of sand falling, then the sound of a clod of dirt thudding to the floor. He fled into the darkness of the tunnel, hearing Lucien's muffled voice:

"But don't go far!"

Peter hurried along the musty tunnel in near total darkness, toward the nothingness an indeterminable distance away. But nothingness seemed to Peter better than time spent in the company of the sinister likes of Lucien.

Chapter Thirty-one
The Siren Call

Peter clambered above ground again from a hole at the base of a tall scraggly pine. He feared, as he looked around, that he was lost in the Deepest Forest. It was a fine mess he was in, all sweaty and dirty and anxious... though it might all have been great fun were it not for the anxiousness, that thing that gnawed and prodded and told him that everything might not be all right, especially in this dreadful place, where trees fell with no one to hear them, and only echoes spoke to one another.

It was dark. It was cool. It was surreal to him, nearly as intriguing as it was frightening. The forest floor, devoid of undergrowth, was carpeted by a heavy layer of long brown pine needles. The trees, all tall pines, were arranged in orderly rows to create a cavernous, stanchioned room, empty, and bordered only by a dark ceiling. Peter moved along one of the rows and the wind whispered to him as he did. This was a neck of the woods he'd formerly avoided. His parents had introduced it to him once, only briefly, and only to tell him of how dangerous it could be for a little boy. His father told him how the CCC had planted the trees during the Great Depression. Peter wasn't exactly sure what the CCC was, nor the Great Depression, but always felt a tremendous sense of despair when he saw trees arranged in rows like these, unvarying fathoms deep, planted by the sullen-faced men he'd seen on the placards at the historical society museum, all leaning on shovels, cigarettes dangling from their lips.

"This way boy, don't lose your way," the wind said. "That's right, just look down and follow the path before you."

It grew darker as Peter moved along, and the trees larger. Peter, in a sudden and fearful haste, moved ever more quickly into the unknown, looking constantly over his shoulders, and from left to right, agreeing with himself more and more that there was more to his adventure than looking for lost crickets in his back yard.

He stumbled and fell, and the soft pine needles were as comfortable as his bed at home. He lay still for a moment and closed his eyes. Then he opened them again, shaking away the languor that caressed him: he was a long way from home. He stood and hurried along.

Ghosts, wild beasts, you name it: if it existed, it was right there, where he was, at that very moment! The trees towered, gargantuans now in both height and girth. There was a sound -- and a light -- flickering in the unforgiving distance. He worked his way between the trees toward it, losing track of the row he'd been following. Laughter emerged from hope and began to echo through the Deepest Forest, and as Peter drew closer, he could see the light was a flickering campfire, set against inky blackness, beyond which surely only the foulest imaginable things dwelt.

Peter crawled toward it on his hands and knees. The voices grew clearer as Peter drew quietly nearer. He dropped and crawled closer, inching along on his stomach like a snake. Bugaboos, like the one in his basement the night before, danced around the fire and drank carelessly from wooden cups, singing nonsense to each other in course voices. Peter kept quiet and watched and listened:

> They laid him brawdawn alanglast bed.
> With a bockalips of finisky fore his feet.
> And a barrowload of guenesis hoer his head!
> *HoHoHo!* I'm the harridan's Flynn again!

"To the water of life and a tipplin' way!" cried the one who'd been singing, and who sounded to Peter like the barber in town when he didn't put his teeth in.

"Lady o' the 'ouse into the craythur again?" asked the other.

"Aye," said the first, sticking his thumb in his mouth and pulling it out with a loud *pop!* "Popped the bung, and another fine evenin' in store!" He held his cup up. "To me glorious lady's spirit!"

By that, Peter pictured him meaning to steal more whisky! He recognized him. It *was* the bugaboo from the night before! It put its cup to its toothless little mouth and quaffed deeply, then began skipping in circles, singing, kicking up pine needles and sloshing himself wet with what Peter could clearly smell was alcohol. Peter thought it a wonder he didn't go up in flames, dancing around a fire so recklessly with his mouth and cup all full of incendiaries. Watching them this way, Peter was reminded of Helmut Gooch, the little fourth-grader that had transferred in -- and then back out again -- during the past school year. His dad had some vague and important job with the government, and Peter wondered who in their right mind would let such an exotic and obvious misfit wander the playground unattended. He was Chinese, tiny and cute-looking as could be, straight from a picture in their social studies book, but spoke three languages, one of which being English laden with a heavy German accent. He was always alone; yet, oddly, he was less of a wraith than Peter – far from it, actually -- because he could cuss you out in all three languages and not leave you wondering what he'd said in any of them. The words just came flying out like punches and karate chops, with the occasional recognizable one interspersed just randomly enough. Pixie Anderson called him Helmut Gook one day – a subtle variant on the softer, more preferred American pronunciation, which had Pixie and a few others thinking he was very clever for having thought to say it.

Helmut got it, too, and from amid the guffaws he retaliated true to form. Mr. Emmett, the gym teacher, had to hustle out and pluck him from near disaster during the middle of one of his flowery, transcultural diatribes. He snatched him up like a football and carried him off while Pixie was struck dumb, squinting and spluttering and generally having a heck of a time, the shock of being set upon by a dirty-mouthed garden cherub having momentarily stolen away his faculties, as well as his thunder. Helmut chawed this and spat that, and slipped and slid along. It was like listening to the boy sing *O Tannenbaum* while chopping vegetables on a wood board, his pie-bald tapestry every bit as effulgent and formidable as it was obtusely profane. Judged by Peter's reckoning, he'd handed Pixie Anderson his head on it. Only Mr. Emmett and playground speculations of Helmut's dad's secret status as a government assassin saved him from retribution.

The bugaboo leapt into an astounding high arc, so peculiar was it that it stopped every thought Peter had in his head. He watched as the bugaboo soared, sipping genteelly from his rude little cup, then slowed at his height's apex and came down again, as graceful as a gymnast, careful not to spill a single drop of his volatile libation. Peter lost him for a second in the trees, what with his senses only slowly returning, but could have sworn his trajectory seemed...

"Ha!"

Peter jerked with a start.

"Ha is right!" shouted the bugaboo, who had landed smack in front of him. "An interloper!"

"Well, where'd 'e come from? A little yoong t' be in this neck o' the woods alone, ain't he?" the other bugaboo said, looking as surprised as Peter and holding his cup just short of his thick, wet lips. They were dressed and looked exactly the same, only this other bugaboo was stouter and more red in the face, and he talked like the chimney-sweep in *Mary Poppins*.

"He's lookin' to steal, ain't ya?" said the bugaboo Peter recognized, reaching to secure his hat on his head. But he wasn't so cute or endearing anymore. He was big (as big as Peter) and rather hard to look at with all his flawed features made so apparent. And that was it: he was startling in an incongruous way, like Helmut Gooch, like looking into a baby carriage and seeing a baby with a cigar in its mouth and whisker stubble. Peter had seen a gag like that on TV once and thought it was funny at the time, but not now. Absurdity has its way of wearing thin.

"Well you steal whisky!" Peter shouted.

"That's not so," said the bugaboo. "I share with me friends."

"You don't have any friends in my house!" exclaimed Peter as he sat up onto his knees then stood.

"Ah, but I do. Now t'aint friendly t' go gettin' upset. I've done nothin' I ain't been asked to do," he said.

"Nobody needs friends like you," said Peter. "And I want you to stay away from my house!"

"But we can be friends, too. And I can show ya a good time. We can pass the days away doin' nothin' at all, watchin' 'em slip by without a care or notice. We're never bored, ol' Frill an' I, and time is meaningless to us. ...Ya do get bored, dontcha? That's because ya feel the passin' of time."

And he wrinkled his brow in an expression of sympathy.

"Oo is this, Flynn?" asked the stout bugaboo.

"Tis the boy of milady," Flynn said, still watching Peter. "Tell ya what I will do," he said to Peter. "I'll give ya this hat for somethin'."

"For what?" asked Peter.

Flynn removed his hat and held it in front of him, baring his wrinkly brown head. "I'll trade ya this hat for your tomorrow," he said with a wink.

Frill began to sing, waving his cup back-and-forth in front of him, but it seemed all he could do to keep from toppling backward into the fire.

"No. I have to steal your hat to make you my slave," Peter said.

"Aw, it doesn't matter how ya get the hat. And slave is such a dirty soundin' word. Why would ya wanta enslave anyone when we can just as easily be friends?"

"Whatta you mean, my tomorrow?" asked Peter, looking past Flynn, into the Deepest Forest.

Flynn smiled. "Why, I can keep ya from havin' t' go t' school. Frill here'll go instead. He'll handle the bullies and keep ya from bein' unhappy." He winked again. "We'll numb ya to the passin' of time."

Peter thought for a few seconds, and a cold breeze blew from the deepest, darkest part of the forest, flickering the fire and whispering: *This way, Peter*.

"I think e's interested, e' is, Flynn," said Frill, who held his cup in the air and began again to sing. "Tiiiiiimmmmmmm Finnegan 'ad a bugaboo..."

"How 'bout we talk a little, whilst I show ya the Deepest Forest," said Flynn, placing his hat back onto his head and holding his cup toward Peter. Peter looked into the cup, then past Flynn, into the blackness of everything and nothing at all, and shuddered with fear and loathing.

"No!" he said, and turned and walked away from the laughing, taunting bugaboos, bugaboos he didn't know and didn't care to.

"Well, ya think about it!" Flynn shouted. "That's right! We'll be 'round when yer ready! We have all the answers here, we do!"

"An' we're always at your service, we are!" added Frill.

Peter put his fingers in his ears and hurried off in the direction leading away from such fools dancing around fires in the middle of nowhere.

Chapter Thirty-two

Post Interrogation

Peter lay on his bed staring at the ceiling. It was past lunchtime and he hadn't eaten, but wasn't hungry anyway. He was too worried about Dillon, who was still unaccounted for. And that wasn't all; he didn't like the thought of Flynn coming and going from his house whenever he wanted. He needed to get that hat!

"Peter!"

A small voice called his name.

"*Peter!* Can I come in?"

Peter rolled off his bed and knelt at the window. Dillon was there, on the sill outside.

"There you are! Where've you been?" asked Peter as he pushed the screen out to let Dillon in.

"The jack-boot thugs had me," Dillon said as he crawled inside. "Been turnin' the screws on me all mornin' long, pretty much since you fell asleep. Made me sit in my underwear for hours on end in an underground cell!"

"Can't imagine that," said Peter, appalled, being himself a very modest person.

"Yeah, psychological torture. Grillin' me with pointless question after pointless question... askin''em this way, then that way, then this, over an' over an' over again. An' you know what? I know more now than when they took me in. More'n they can say for themselves."

"Whatta you mean?" asked Peter.

"One was holdin' a clipboard... threatened t' hit me with it a couple a' times. Anyway, I saw a name on it."

"A name? Whose name?"

"Icarus Whistler."

"Who's Icarus Whistler?"

"A blue jay."

"A bird?"

"That's right."

Peter rubbed the top of his head as he thought. "Well," he said, "Lucien was awfully interested in birds when he talked to me. Now maybe I know why. I'll bet..."

"They talked to you, too?" Dillon asked.

"Um-hm," Peter said. "But not in my underwear."

Dillon's jaw dropped.

Peter continued: "Lucien said, 'I'm a bird...'"

"*Eh-hem*," Dillon cleared his throat. "Ah, hold on a minute," he said with a peevish little chuckle. "Not in your underwear?"

"No," said Peter. They stared at one another for a second or two. "I didn't know bugs even wore underwear."

"*Ho!* What's the matter with you?"

"What!?" replied Peter. "Sorry, what's so bad about that?"

"Oh, *come on*. What sorta bug doesn't wear underwear?"

Peter shrugged. Why all the fuss? he wondered. It wasn't the worst thing he could think of. Shoot, he wouldn't wear underwear himself if it weren't for his mom keeping track. She might be guilty more often than not of letting the reigns go slack, but not when it came to the weekly tally of underwear! Never mind clean shirts or socks, but you could bet on a bleach-smelling pair of briefs for every day of the week, and a marshaling like none other to see that you were wearing them!

"That's not important," he said to Dillon. "What's important is what I was tryin' to say about Lucien, which was..."

"Hold on, hold on, not so fast," Dillon interrupted. "Y' gotta be kidding, right?"

"What?" replied Peter.

"Y' know the purpose a' underwear is t' keep your clothes clean, don't cha? As well as other folks' furniture if y' plan t' sit on it. It's an issue of hygiene."

Peter just stared. Dillon tossed his head in exasperation.

"So you're sayin' they didn't send y' off like some floozy, holdin' your clothes?" he asked.

Peter was steadily shaking his head. Dillon watched, then looked down and touched his forehead and started counting slowly to ten while rocking "Mr. Angry" in his so-called cradle... an old technique he remembered learning from his Mama to keep Mr. Angry from climbing out his mouth. He was committed now to shortening Mr. Angry's leash. He muttered to himself along the way about being a "melody-maker" and "not a fighter" and "jus' doin' what any good citizen would've done"... which Peter assumed to mean under the circumstances. That would have put it along the same lines as their new-found roles as Queen's personal champions earlier, with Dillon's sudden inclusion into the ranks of "good citizenry" being a form of battlefield promotion – not to be confused with lesser forms of sheer convenience -- since Peter had never known Dillon to ever agree with any of the other good citizens before.

Peter was quick to recognize it all as such only because he was himself a little suspicious of *ad hoc* promotions, having been a victim of one in the past: the day the teacher had to literally drag a girl down to the office for throwing an intractable hissy during class, and told Peter to write down the names of anyone who left their desk while she was gone. ...Thirteen kids, all defying him to write their names down, even the lowliest of them, because there could be nothing lowlier than a snitch and everyone knew it.

When Dillon was done muttering and counting, he exhaled slowly. "*Ohhh*-kay," he said. "Well... Anyway... Ah... Get down, you! ...Ahhh... *Son-of-a*... I'm alright, I'm alright... Ah... What was I gonna say? ...Aw, never mind!"

"Yeah," said Peter, "never mind, 'cause I got an idea."

Chapter Thirty-three

Dangerous Games

"What are you, some sorta tweety-bird?"

One would have thought Squeak liked the abuse.

"Aw, cut it out Icarus, I could've died," he said.

Squeak heaved as he struggled for breath, panting forcefully, hunched forward with wings akimbo.

"I don't think you got a feather on your chest!" scolded Icarus. "Do it like this, you candy apple!" Icarus breathed deeply several times, then puffed his cheeks and darted at break-neck speed into the stratosphere. Up, up, up, he went, until he had completely disappeared. Squeak and the others watched in awed silence then looked at one another. They waited. No Icarus. Their looks grew anxious.

"He's done it this time," said Squeak, shaking his head ominously.

"I think he made it all the way to the sun," said another.

"No. Wait. Here he comes!"

A speck appeared high in the sky. Squeak and the others strained to watch. It was him. Icarus was shooting earthbound, his feathers trailing limp in a lifeless free-fall.

"Icarus!"

The others flew up to meet him as he sped downward, completely unconscious.

"Icarus! Icarus!"

Icarus fell. The others scattered as Icarus whizzed past them like a rocket, and they turned to watch, waiting for the inevitable: plumage scattered across the meadow. Such tragedies were known to occur amongst birds, when some foolhardy fellow went higher than they should have. The others circled and squawked uselessly as they watched. Then, suddenly, Icarus awoke and spread his wings. He beat them in slow, powerful strokes as he fought the shear of rushing wind... and, in the instant before impact, he slowed, grazing the tops of the meadow grass as he swooped through a dramatic, upward arc to alight in a nearby tree.

The others all hurried down. "You're nuts!" they cried. "Yes!"

And that was their unanimous opinion.

"What happened?" Squeak asked.

"Don't know," said Icarus, still somewhat dazed. "Must've passed out. I've never gone so high in my life. I think I saw... The Creator."

"Whoa! Man, you actually passed out! Yes! Yes!"

The others cawed their assent.

Squeak, once again emboldened, breathed deeply, just as Icarus had done, then suddenly shot upward... more like a rubber band than a rocket, though, because he turned back a few seconds later.

"Oh, man, I think I almost passed out," he said.

"No way, tweety-pie. I don't think so. Not even close," said Icarus. "Go on, try again."

"I dunno, Icarus. I'm not that crazy."

"Yeah, me neither," mumbled another.

Everyone became very quiet while busily averting their eyes from Icarus's demanding stare.

"What, none of you can hang with me?" Icarus looked from one to the other, all of whom just continued looking down at their talons. "What a bunch a' tweeties. See you around *girls*, I'll be at Boog's."

Icarus started off when Squeak called to him, "Wait! Icarus! Look!"

Icarus turned back with a quick flourish and landed on a branch to watch with the others as Peter busied himself on the porch behind his house. He was spreading peanut butter onto a milk carton with a butter knife, then reached into a plastic bag full of bread and pulled out a slice. He crumbled it carefully onto the porch and worked the crumbs into the peanut butter with his fingers, then went toward the back of the yard to hang the whole thing by a string from a tree limb.

"Manna!" cried Icarus, and he and the others all began a noisy clamor.

They cawed from the boughs of the trees where they had flocked, barely able to wait for Peter to finish and leave. Icarus was boldest among them, and flew to within feet of where Peter worked, shrieking to hurry him along.

"Is that him?" Peter asked.

"Sure is," said Dillon as Peter hastily fashioned a knot.

"Why can't I understand 'em?"

"Speed freaks. That's the way the young hot-shots talk these days. Can't understand 'em unless they're singin'. I think they confuse each another. Best I can figure, Icarus and his posse are a bit of an embarrassment t' their flock. His Ma and Pa're always scoldin' him in front of everyone."

"Well, let's move away and see what he does," said Peter as he cinched the knot tight.

He wiped his hands on his shorts, and he Dillon walked nonchalantly back to the house... then ran, once inside, to Peter's room to watch through his window. Peter pulled his curtains closed and peered out from a corner. The greedy birds swarmed the feeder immediately, fighting one another for spots on the perch Peter had made from a pencil. The milk carton swung and bounced back and forth in the tumult.

"By golly!" said Dillon. "Just look at 'em, ravenous gluttons that they are. You'd think they hadn't eaten in a week. They're gonna knock it off the string!"

"Hope not," said Peter. "It's sure not hard to tell which one's Icarus, is it?"

There was a frenzied racket of clamoring birds loud enough to be heard a mile away.

"That peanut butter's like candy to 'em," said Dillon.

Peter watched Icarus, brash and aggressive in comparison to the others. He whisked back and forth from the nearby trees, displacing his friends from the perch whenever he took the notion for seconds, thirds and fourths.

"Looks like we got 'em all together," said Peter. "We'll follow 'em when they get done."

Chapter Thirty-four

Proteus

"**H**ey, Icarus, you see how much I ate? Sheesh, I think I ate more'n anyone. Check out my gut."

Squeak lifted his feathers to show a very scrawny stomach, his torso resembling, of all things, a bird cage.

"I saw you, peckin' away like some spastic chicken," replied Icarus, his eyes half closed. "Sheesh, and wipe your chin, you drooling slob, before you make us all sick to our stomachs."

Squeak wiped his chin while the others snickered. He had quite a mess on his face. He looked at his wing, then licked the tip and wiped again at his face, then shook his feathers.

"Hey! *Hey!* Watch it Squeak, you moron! You're gonna get it all over us!"

Squeak was quietly licking the rest of his feathers, but stopped. "Hey, Icarus, why are those two watching us like that?"

Icarus opened an eye. "Where?"

Squeak pointed to the ground behind the wood pile. "There. Look."

Peter crouched, along with Dillon behind the wood pile, and watched the birds, all of whom stared back.

"It's that little retard, Hopper. Look!"

Icarus opened both eyes. "Hopper, with his new boyfriend!"

The birds all fluttered back and forth between the trees, filling them with jeers and derisive laughter. Peter and Dillon maintained their not-so-secret position with the dawning realization that their cover was blown.

"Hey, Hopper! Who's your new boyfriend? Hey! Hey! How about you play your magic fiddle for us!" shouted Icarus, prompting a whole new a barrage of laughter, taunts and jibes.

"Yeah, Hopper, you stink!" That from Squeak.

"Shut up! *Shut up!*" began Dillon, when Peter stopped him.

"Dillon, calm down. Remember? We have a plan?"

The plan was to quietly follow the birds. What they hadn't anticipated was the problem becoming one of who would be following whom. To these particular birds, hard pressed by the rigors of indolence, being troublesome was economical. It was as easy and predictable and as natural a thing in the world for them to do, especially in terms of expenditure of energy, of which they were notoriously stingy. Icarus and the others were all willing to apply themselves for the sake of a laugh – and little else -- making the victimization of others to that end among their sole justifications for physical exertion... that, and a thrill or a belly full of junk-food, as we've already seen. What with one moving always with an eye on the others, their actions were more akin to knee-jerks than any willful, cognizant effort, more or less like the amoeba Peter never found under his microscope, one big fluctuating cloud, tearing across the sky. And so it was in this case, a flock of otherwise lazy birds fully engaged in a minimal endeavor, led to it by their tiny brainstems and juvenile proclivities. Peter followed as the birds followed him toward the road, then back to the yard, then to the road, then back to the yard... needless to say, it was slow going, as well as upsetting to the plan.

"First one to bring me Hopper gets an attaboy!"

Icarus upped the ante, and all the birds responded by swooping down in turn on Peter as he and Dillon walked along the gravel road. Peter was afraid they were trying to shear off his earlobes and peck his eyes out, an idea that suddenly came to him based on the morbid blatherings of Pixie Anderson. Pixie had seen it in a movie on cable TV: once they got your eyes, you were inexplicably dead, same as a zombie bite, or having your heart burst from sheer fright, or hitting the ground when you were falling in a dream. These were laws of physics, which were sound in principle, especially if you'd ever seen or heard of them in a movie. Pixie claimed birds had beaks like tin-snips, and used them as such during killing binges, and so Peter began to run with Dillon on his shoulder.

"He does the color blue something shameful," said a breathless Dillon to Peter as he dodged the dive-bombing birds.

"I've seen 'em before," replied Peter. "Carryin' on. My grandpa threw a softball at 'em once... Watch your eyes!"

Just then, Dillon was plucked from Peter's shoulder and taken aloft as a plaything for Icarus and his friends. They tossed him from one to the other, soaring and swooping high in the sky beneath the brightly dappled clouds. Dillon fluttered in several useless attempts to escape, but Icarus or one of the others were always right there, ready to snatch him again. Peter ran along on the ground below, hollering up at them.

"Let him go! Let him go!"

But they were too fast and had benefit of the unimpeded airway. And soon they had disappeared across the meadow.

Chapter Thirty-five
Dillon In The Well

The Barnsworths were one of the oldest families in the county. Pops Barnsworth, notorious renegade, was said to have run liquor for the Purple Gang, back and forth across the Detroit River from Canada on a sled, back in the days when the river froze. But that was only the well-known and unofficial buzz, which happened to coexist alongside many other myths and quasi-truths. His verifiable exploits, though, made a worthy enough and prominent footnote in Wexford county history on their own... either that or they were a convenient and dubiously presented blemish which may or may not have been preserved solely for the benefit of antiquity, depending on who one asked and how deeply they delved into county politics. And there was quite literally a footnote written on a historical placard in town, ostensibly to show the Civilian Conservation Corps hard at work extinguishing, and then later replanting the forest, their work made necessary, this notation adds, by the "criminal negligence of one, Pops Barnsworth." No doubt, it was loaded statements like this that made people wonder who was actually most guilty of starting fires. Pops, as this enlightening yet curiously ambivalent footnote makes clear, dabbled with corn-mash whisky and a pot-still during prohibition... until it blew up and started a conflagration that nearly wiped out the farm and surrounding countryside. At least one person was blown to smithereens by it, presumably Pops, since the pieces were "too small to be identifiable and he was never seen or heard from again." As to whether Pops was worse for being criminally inept, or just being a criminal, Peter never cared, because he and those who shared his view soaked it up with an awe so vastly immeasurable that they couldn't even find expression in sympathy because of it, let alone rage or indignation. How could there be any assignment of guilt when they imagined the incident likely the most extraordinary thing ever to happen in any history anywhere? To them, Pops Barnsworth was right up there with Paul Bunyan and Johnny Appleseed... or even both in one, as some of the more astute ones tended to think. Kids like Peter never even gave a thought to the subtler and bleaker implications... unless you counted the stories of Pops roaming the Deepest Forest as a ghost, looking for his missing parts.

But that was kid stuff, and a whole other story.

Rather than sudden and complete annihilation, the big farm itself came down slowly from its zenith to end up little more than a tillable plot a single old woman could tend for her own pleasure... that old woman being Peter's friend, Mrs. Barrow. All the land, which people and fires could only temporarily efface, grew things now which were in Peter's estimation way more valuable and interesting than food: the old abandoned well for one. It was a standing column of fieldstone mortared together just the way great, great-granddaddy Barnsworth had left it so many years ago, overgrown with trees and brush now near where the original Barnsworth homestead had stood before the fire. The wood crank-and-pulley mechanism that lowered the bucket to draw water had decayed and collapsed into the well long ago, and it was dark down there, rumored to be *miles* deep and haunted by oddities from the tortured dreams of madmen. For generations, scores of every manner of children took their turns listening at the well to what all readily agreed were eerie echoes of anguished cries from the bowels of Hell. Icarus dove, fully aware of the well's reputation, cleaving the air steadily toward it, holding

Dillon.

He swooped and dropped him in!

Down, down, down Dillon fell, disoriented and unable to beat his wings to any effect, careening off the sides and tumbling like a whirligig all along the way. Darkness quickly consumed him, and the temperature dropped as he fell, further and further, until...

Splash!

Dillon clambered to the water's surface -- he hoped it was only water! -- and stood atop it but briefly before his tiny feet pierced through the surface tension and he floundered again, gasping and flapping. He had never been in water before. Water was a frightening place for magicadas, all full of primal beasts of low intelligence and biting mouths -- especially in *these* dark waters, teeming with the unthinkable abominations that washed out occasionally onto the creek bank -- bulgy blind eyes and colorless skin, lacking in compunction and completely ignorant of any social graces.

"HEELLPP! ...Gulp. ...*HELP!*"

Flailing in sheer and utter terror, Dillon somehow found a solid surface in the pitch-darkness, and he stood. But even standing, left was right and up was down, and try as he might, he could not orient himself. He shivered and sneezed.

"*HELLLP!*" he cried.

Only an echo replied. Then another and another and another.

"Someone, HEELLPP!" (omeone, ELP, ELP, omeone, ELP, one.)

Three *plunks* sounded into the water across from him. Too scared to stay still, afraid to bring any more attention to himself by shouting, Dillon began groping his way along, hands waving blindly in front of him. He heard a *click* and a *sploosh* and the constant sound of the trickle of water. And echoes. Everything had an echo. He heard a *blurp* and a *hiss* and moved with all the speed he could manage in the dark. He thought to fly, and leapt, but struck his head on something, only to fall back again into the water. He heard another *splish* as he flailed about, then stumbled forward onto an invisible shore. He thought he heard muffled sounds.

Voices, he thought.

He moved toward them.

Intelligent life, he dared hope.

He moved faster. ...There was a light! ...Faster. ...Brighter! ...He stumbled. Three more splishes. Brighter! ...Faster! ...Dillon burst into the light of day.

"...And get this, he says to start calling him *Mister* Pasquale from now on!"

Dillon panted in relief, although relief only applied to his good fortune in escaping the well. Otherwise, the voice coming from the weeds ahead sounded like that of Algernon Fess.

"You hear about Gasper LaRue?" he heard Algernon ask.

"How's someone get their head stuck in a can?" asked another voice.

"He said he smelled Cracker Jacks inside," said Algernon.

"He eats that crap?" asked the other.

And Boog Barrow! thought Dillon, crouching as he listened and suddenly more than a little scared. Cats like Boog and Algernon were known to kill bugs for fun!

"He said the kid he lives with got him hooked," said Algernon.

"Sheesh, what an idiot," muttered Boog.

Silence. ...A loud yawn.

Trees shaded the place where they were. There was water running from underground, from where Dillon had just escaped, into a brisk flowing creek. Algernon and Boog talked casually from somewhere in the tall grass.

"Hey," said Algernon, "I saw that little priss at the barber shop again today..."

Boog chuckled.

"...prancin' back and forth with that bell around his neck." Algernon used lisps and tinny S's to imply some sort of sissy. Dillon listened as they both laughed.

Silence again.

The sound of a screen door banging shut in the near distance. One of the cats began to sing, horribly off key, "Ma-ry had a lit-tal-lamb, lit-tal-lamb, lit-TAL-lamb..."

It was Boog.

"So, you goin' at it again tonight?" asked Algernon.

"Of course, it's *my* spotlight now. ...Its fleeeeeeeeece... Its fleeeece... It's fleece... Was whiiiiite as snow." Boog finished as a dolorous bass in the style of a barbershop quartet.

"Yeah, you own the night now, Boog. Just give it time and it'll catch on."

"I'm not worried," replied Boog, without a hint of worry. Then he broke into a discordant volley of arpeggios.

"What're you gonna do with... ah... you know who?"

"*Who?*" gushed Boog in a sarcastic whisper.

"You know," said Algernon, lowering his own voice. "...The cricket."

He said "the cricket" so quietly that Dillon barely heard him.

"Let him rot," said Boog.

Dillon's eyes popped wide open.

"Just *leave* him in there?" Algernon asked.

"Why not?" said Boog. "With him outta my way..."

"That'd be..." gulp, "like murder!"

"And maybe you should see if you can borrow Tinker's little bell! You're a killer. I'm a killer. Whatta you think?"

"Killing and murder are not the same things," said Algernon.

"Only if you say so!" snarled Boog.

"...You would do *that* just to hear yourself sing?"

"Shut up, *pussy* cat!"

There was the sudden sound of a skirmish in the weeds, with grunts and hisses, and the plucking, ripping sounds Boog made on the back of Mrs. Barrow's couch.

And then it stopped. Dillon panicked and flew away.

Chapter Thirty-six
Scylla

Old Mrs. Barrow owned the house where Boog lived, on the other side of the meadow, away from Peter, some distance and across another road from where the Barnsworth homestead once stood, in an area of expansive acreage also owned by her. She was actually a member of the landed aristocracy, much to the displeasure of the rotund and ridiculous Mrs. Jenkins -- wife of the grocer, crabby Mr. Jenkins -- as well as the other dilly-dallies of the local Inner Wheel, all of whom liked to gather and reduce their social club's venerable mission to that of a snooty sorority. They didn't like Mrs. Barrow because they considered her a straight-talking rustic, and she shunned them as useless gossips and gadflies: "Haughty fish in a little pond," she liked to say. These ladies did manage to secure a millage to nurture their pet project, a wondrously hermetic boondoggle they dubbed the Lake Wexford Society for the Preservation of Antiquity and Historic Self-Guided Tours, where they had an old restored house and barn with historic placards (as previously described); home decorations, replete with quality antique furnishings, right down to the quilted bedcovers and worn leather brogans bedside; sterling silver flatware and Delft Blue dinner setting, including teacups and saucers, set out as if for a meal (although Peter was certain pioneers ate with their fingers and a pocket knife, and maybe a spoon from time to time); and a display of farm implements as ordinary as any to be seen throughout the entire United States of America... or, so was the word on the playground after one boring field trip. It was far less interesting than just going over to Mrs. Barrow's house and seeing the same things, what with the nosey biddies all constantly skulking and hovering about like they owned the place, admonitory fingers at the ready.

(For anyone interested, it could be visited from noon to three, on Mondays, Wednesdays and Thursdays.)

Mrs. Barrow, for that matter, was *the* member of the landed aristocracy, since she owned more land than any single person or family in three counties. She, a red barn and her house, and all the fallow acreage were all that remained of the legacy though; along with the well and a field of yellow daffodils surrounding the barn. Peter always liked the way the red and yellow and green, and blue of the sky came together so beautifully in that place during the spring-time of every year. Springtime, you see, could come and go in a day, what with the snow's duress pressing nearly into June, and the color-ed daffodils bid a timely "good riddance" to winter's drab. Peter always liked looking for that special day.

Mrs. Barrow was a Barnsworth -- the last of the Barnsworths -- transfigured by marriage, and then again by the eventual loss of her dearly departed husband, Mr. Hurley Barrow, who used to like to sit on his porch and chew tobacco. And spit. But Peter had never met him, though he thought he might have liked him. (He was long gone before Peter was born: Mrs. Barrow just liked to talk about him.)

Mrs. Barrow was outside, a very kindly lady toward Peter, though she tended to speak too loudly, and with hair a subtle but baffling shade of blue, except nearest the scalp, where it was distinctly gray. She was facing away from the road and the front of the house, water-ing a little garden full of tomatoes, and corn, and green beans and pumpkins. Peter and Dillon helped themselves up her red brick walk, which was nicely edged and manicured. She always did a very nice job of things, considering her limitations. Mrs. Barrow was nearly deaf and blind, and so was startled when Peter tapped her arm from behind.

"Ooh!" she said. Mrs. Barrow's face glowed white behind thick, black-rimmed spectacles. They acted as magnifying glasses, and made her look like a big bug with huge eyes.

"I brought my friend," said Peter. He held out Dillon on the palm of his hand. Mrs. Barrow squinted to see, looking very closely.

"A grasshopper, huh?"

"Magicada," said Peter. Mrs. Barrow looked up and squinted in response, implying that she hadn't heard him well enough -- which was just as well -- a fortunate near-miss, in fact, since drawn-out discussions about insect taxonomy with nearly deaf persons could be time-consuming and Peter was in a hurry. He decided it might be easier to stick to the facts as she knew them. "I was just wondering if you had any crickets around here!" he said, yelling this time to be sure she heard the question, and taking the opportunity to come directly to the point.

"Crickets?" she asked. "Oh, sure, I suppose I have lots of crickets. Haven't heard any lately, though. Course, I don't hear too well anyway," she finished, muttering the last bit to herself.

"Well, do you mind if we have a look around the yard?" asked Peter, trying to speak only as loudly as she did.

Mrs. Barrow squinted again and shook her head with a distressed look, flicking at her ear with a bony finger.

"DO YOU MIND IF WE LOOK AROUND FOR A CRICKET?" shouted Peter.

It was always far more difficult to talk to her outside.

"Help yourself," she said with a wave and a smile, causing the stream of water pouring from her hose to dance in front of her and nearly douse Peter. She turned to direct it on her already rather large pumpkins. Peter walked up and knelt to thump one.

"WOW," he said, "THESE ARE GONNA BE HUGE!"

Mrs. Barrow smiled, "Well, all they need is lots a' water. You and your dad can come get one for Halloween. I'll grow that one special for you."

Peter thumped it again, smiling. "THANKS," he said, then turned and wandered off toward the back of the house.

"Halloween?" said Dillon.

"Oh, it's really cool. We dress up and go around and get candy from the people in town. My dad wears a mask and looks like a wrinkly old lady. It's really fun. Can't wait to go with you."

Dillon was quiet.

"Don't know," he said finally. "By the time that pumpkin's as big as she says, sounds like it'll be pretty late in the season. 'Specially in these parts."

Dillon didn't know any insects who'd been to a Halloween party.

"Yeah, but that's okay," said Peter. "...Why?"

"Oh, nothin'," said Dillon. (Drear thoughts of Oblivion had snuck into his head.) "Just lookin' forward to it, that's all."

Peter laughed. "Maybe you can rent a tux and go as the Maestro."

"Speakin' of which," said Dillon, "he's gotta be round here somewhere. Sounded like Boog was holdin' him prisoner."

"He said 'let him rot?'" asked Peter, aghast.

"That's what he said, all right... an' all because *he* wants to sing!"

They continued on in silence, shaking their heads. Mrs. Barrow's clothesline was there, with her unmentionables hanging limp in the heat. The two looked at one another and giggled. Peter walked to the house and turned a few stones over in the flower bed, as well as the cement rain guards that sat beneath the gutter spouts on each corner of the house. All they found was a toad underneath, who implored, "Put it back! Put it back!"

Peter put it back.

There was a coop further out back, where Mrs. Barrow kept a few chickens. Peter watched them milling around, doing what it was that chickens did all day, then headed toward them.

"Whoa, where ya goin'?" asked Dillon.

"T' check out there."

"Not a good idea," Dillon said. "There's a banty of the worst sort."

"Jackie Gobble-Korn," said Peter.

Dillon laughed, "Yeah, that's him. Wouldn't call him that to his face, though."

Peter blinked in sudden and genuine bewilderment. "Whatta y' mean?" he asked. "*I* gave him that name."

"Yeah, well, you gave him *a* name, and he's never forgiven you for it. His real name's Jack Cockalorum and everyone snickers behind his back about the Jackie Gobble-Korn thing. He's in charge a' the hens, see? Thinks he's a real tough-guy. Always lookin' for a fight."

"...He doesn't *like* me?" asked Peter, pointing to himself in disbelief. And it was a genuine disbelief, considering the fact that Peter considered himself virtually a parent... if not, at least a Godparent, or some other sort of surrogate. He was there, for cripe's sake, on the day Jackie Gobble-Korn was hatched! Another hot summer day, as he recalled, just like this one, when he'd simply hoped for some ice-cream, or lemonade, or some other form of refreshing largesse... as well as maybe a screwdriver or a chisel to knock out a marble or two from the cement alongside Mrs. Barrow's driveway.

"No," replied Dillon.

And what an apt way to punctuate Peter's astonishment! Peter might eventually learn that this, like one of his many sighs, was yet another of life's punctuation marks, less emphatic and surely less commonplace than a sigh, but more singular in what it implied. Peter looked into the coop, and that said it all: Impudent little "Jack" was standing there, glaring at him with his chest puffed out.

"Well, I was only nine when I named him that. Mrs. Barrow thought it was nice," Peter said, looking apologetically at Dillon.

"Forget about it," said Dillon.

Peter turned away from the coop. "You should see him freak out when someone spreads a little corn around, greedy little bugger." Peter was suddenly filled with scorn. "He runs ahead a' the hens and keeps 'em away as best as he can. Takes care of himself before anyone else, that's for sure. Jack Cockalorum, great leader of hens!"

"Never mind," said Dillon.

They worked their way around front. Peter stooped to look under the porch, then knelt. There were nothing but spiders and cobwebs. "Gee, hope he didn't end up under here."

"Yeah," said Dillon with a shudder. "End up is right. If he's here, he ain't makin' no noise."

"How're we supposed to find the Maestro *unless* he makes some noise?" asked Peter as he stood, brushing at the blades of grass stuck to his knees.

"Good question," said Dillon. "I really doubt he's outside, or he'd still be conductin'. Betcha he's somewhere inside."

Peter wiped his brow with the back of his wrist. "Well," he said, "I could ask Mrs. Barrow for somethin' to drink."

Dillon snapped his fingers and pointed at Peter as though he were very clever. Peter mounted the creaky porch and knocked on the screen door, *tap-tap-tap-tap-tap.*

No answer. He heard Mrs. Barrow inside, talking. "Maybe she's on the phone," he said to Dillon.

Dillon shrugged.

Peter rapped harder -- *Bangety-Bangety-Bangety-Bang!* -- the door bouncing open a little with each bang, like a boxer hitting a speed-bag, and that's exactly what Peter likened himself to whenever he knocked on it that way. Mrs. Barrow stopped talking and stepped out a few seconds later from the kitchen. She stood, crouched and squinting at Peter, who had his face pressed against the screen, hands bridged across his forehead to see inside.

"Oh! Well, come on in," said Mrs. Barrow.

Peter opened the door and stepped in.

"Can we... *eh-hem*... can I have a drink, please?"

"A drink? Sure. What would you like?"

Mrs. Barrow stopped in front of Peter with her hands clasped at her chest.

"Hmm. ...Ah, milk would be good."

"Oh, milk! Good choice. So good for you. I'll be right back." Mrs. Barrow turned, mumbling as she hobbled away. Milk was really not very good on a hot day, and Peter knew that, but had a feeling Mrs. Barrow might be impressed by the choice. He sat down on an upholstered chair in the living room, a very large chair in which he chose not to sit all the way back. Its cloth fabric was colored shades of brown and green, and would surely have swallowed him whole had he sat all the way back, so he sat forward and let his feet dangle, and kicked the chair with his heels, making a steady rhythm of solid thumps -- *Thump. Thump-thump. Thump. Thump-thump. Thump. Thump-thump*.

There was a single, muffled chirp in response to this little *basso continuo* of his.

Peter stopped swinging his legs and looked toward the staircase to the second floor, then at Dillon. Dillon nodded. Peter got up and crept across the living room. Mrs. Barrow was talking again, still in the kitchen, but as he nearly reached the first step, she stopped abruptly. Peter lurched back to his chair on tip-toes.

"Here you are," she said as she emerged from the kitchen. She handed Peter a glass of milk and smiled. The glass was full, right to the top, more milk than Peter could drink in two days. He smiled and took a sip. Mrs. Barrow continued to stand and smile with her hands clasped at her chest.

"Oh," said Peter. "If you have anything to do, just go right ahead and do it. Don't mind us."

"No bother," said Mrs. Barrow, and she stood and smiled.

Peter took another small sip and looked around the room. He smiled back at Mrs. Barrow as he swallowed. "Oh," he said, "I thought you might be on the phone, or something."

"On the phone?"

"Yeah, we heard you talkin' to someone in there."

"Talking? ...Oh! I was just talkin' to Boog."

And then Boog sauntered out of the kitchen. He strolled across the living room, then stopped, mid-stride, and dropped to the floor, breaking into an enormous, tremulous stretch. He was at least four feet long, from toe to razor-sharp toe, claws flared like stilettos and made plain enough to see. He yawned a cavernous yawn, at least six-hundred pointed white teeth gleaming, then looked at Peter and Dillon with a languid wink and a smile.

"Yikes!" chirped Dillon, which to Mrs. Barrow was barely audible.

Boog closed his eyes, sinister smirk intact, and nodded sleepily as he breathed a loud, churning purr.

Peter took another sip of his milk.

"Oh..." he began, when the chirping started again. Boog's eyes snapped open and his purring stopped. He looked up the stairs, then at Peter, his cat's eyes narrowing.

Peter said to Mrs. Barrow, "Do you have any cookies?"

Boog sat alert.

"Cookies?" asked Mrs. Barrow.

"Um-hm," said Peter, nodding and striking his most disarming smile.

"Well, I have the refrigerated kind I can cut with a butter knife and cook on a baking pan. It'll take a few minutes, though."

"Oh, that's all right," replied Peter. "I'll wait."

"What about your supper?"

"Oh, my mom won't mind."

"You sure?"

"Pretty sure."

"All right, then. I'll be back in a few minutes," said Mrs. Barrow. "But just a few. Don't want your mom sore at me for spoilin' your supper." She continued muttering as she walked away.

"I told you about those refrig..." Dillon began.

"Never mind," said Peter, and held a finger to his lips. "*Shh!*"

He waited until he heard the rustle of a pan in the kitchen, then got up again and tip-toed toward the stairs. Boog raced ahead of him, growling and rumbling like thunder in a coffee can. Peter stopped halfway. ...The chirping began again. Peter moved toward Boog. Boog barred his way with a steady barrage of menacing sounds. ...Peter inched closer. ...He paused. Boog curled his lip and with bared teeth let go a wavering, undulating frequency of unearthly quality. The chirping stopped. Peter held his breath. This cat was more than a masterful intimidator.

Peter lunged and then it was on!

Peter leapt! Boog revved and swiped with a burst of noise and rage! Peter was hit! And just like the day in the meadow when he was felled by Pixie Anderson, the fog of battle dampened his wits to show it all to him in a series of slow motion snapshots as he dashed up the stairs:

Adrenaline. Chirping from a room at the far end of a hallway. A tarnished, antique doorknob. The knob in his hand. Turn it. The knob *in* his hand! Wiggle and jam it back! Twist. The door pops inward. A crack. A creak. Darkness. Staleness. The smell. A seldom used room. A tomb. Vapors from a tomb.

"How long since anyone's slept in here?" he wondered aloud.

"Over there!" cried Dillon.

The chirping started again. Peter bounded over the bed and skidded on the hardwood floor to the corner. Heavy red drapes covered the window all the way to the floor. Boog leapt and attached himself to Peter's leg, wrapping his claws around and latching into him with every available point, back legs pumping and rasping in a murderous fury!

Stifled scream. ...Kick, kick! ...Reach down. ...Grab the cat. ...Throw him! ...Scratching, skidding into the wall beside the old wardrobe. ...*KLUMP!* ...Pull back the drapes. ...Not much time. ...Hurry!

"Sorry, Maestro, no time for introductions!"

Peter scooped him up as Boog came screaming toward him again. Peter bounded across the bed, then to the floor and out the door, jerking it shut behind him.

The knob came off in his hand again.

Chapter Thirty-seven
Charybdis

Peter was back in real time, the fog of battle now lifted and his formerly dulled sense of corporeal self acutely piqued. He was sitting again in the upholstered chair when Mrs. Barrow brought a plate full of cookies in from the kitchen.

"Hope these don't spoil your supper," she said in a stern voice.

"I don't think so," said Peter, rubbing his wounded leg in a deliberately obvious way. Mrs. Barrow set the plate down and noticed.

"What's wrong?" she asked, then stooped to have a closer look. She took Peter's ankle in her cold, gnarled hand and pulled it closer for a more thorough inspection through her gigantic spectacles. Red stripes crissed and crossed and glowed along Peter's calf, each slowly oozing blood.

"How'd *that* happen?" she asked in her loud voice as she looked up and blinked.

"Boog," said Peter.

"*Boog?*"

"Yeah, I just walked up to give 'em a little pet and he hissed and clawed me."

"He *did?!*"

"Yeah."

Mrs. Barrow stared through her big glasses.

"Well, I never! ...Where is he now?"

"He ran upstairs. ...I think he went into the room at the end of the hall. I pulled the door shut so he couldn't come back out." Peter held the doorknob out to her.

She took it and looked at it. "Why that...! Come with me," she said.

Peter followed her up the stairs. She led him into her bathroom, down the hallway opposite to where Boog was. She opened a medicine cabinet behind a big mirror over the sink and picked through the things until she found an amber glass bottle.

"Iodine," she announced, holding it up.

"...What for?" asked Peter.

"Those scratches, of course," answered Mrs. Barrow as she unscrewed the top. "Don't want 'em gettin' infected. Sit there on the toilet," she said, and held the bottle upside-down on a ball of cotton, which quickly turned brown.

"...Oh... I think I'll be all right," said Peter quickly, leery of the old-fashioned, cold-steel-and-sunshine brand of medicine Mrs. Barrow was so fond of mentioning in nearly all their conversations. (She had been a nurse's assistant, once upon a time, "at the old Receivin' Hospital in Detroit.")

"There's no need for all that," Peter added. "You keep it. You might need it for yourself."

"Eh?"

"It's okay, you don't need to do that... Ow!"

"Nonsense. Now hold still."

Mrs. Barrow dabbed the brown cotton against Peter's scratches as she clutched his leg by the ankle.

"*Owwww!*" cried Peter, writhing and jerking.

"Now, now," said Mrs. Barrow, "be brave. What doesn't kill you makes you stronger. Believe me, I know. I was a nurse's assistant, you know, way back when, at the old Receivin' Hospital in Detroit. Treated the likes of the Fords and the Dodges. Big drinkers, they were, used to sweat it out in the sauna boxes after their binges."

Peter twisted in agony as Mrs. Barrow held the iodine on his leg. "Ow-*wow-wow-wow!* That *really* stings!"

"I know, I know. ...Done," she announced triumphantly. She released Peter's leg and tossed the brown cotton into a waste pail beside the vanity. "A little triple antibiotic and you're on your way."

She picked through the medicine cabinet and found a crinkly tube of ointment. She stooped and snatched up Peter's leg again and slathered it with brusque, confident strokes. "There," she said, smiling with an almost forgotten satisfaction. "Still got it. ...Now, about Boog. ...Boog! Where are you? ...You go on downstairs, Peter, and have yourself a few cookies... no more'n a few, though. I'll be down soon as I find that naughty kitty."

Chapter Thirty-eight
Icarus Whistler Comes Crashing Down

Peter was sitting in the upholstered chair again when Mrs. Barrow came down the stairs, holding Boog out in front of her as if he smelled bad. His face was pinched into a silly look of chagrin, with ears back and eyes nothing but slits. Peter chewed his cookie while Mrs. Barrow walked by and began tapping Boog briskly on the head, scolding, "*No* Boog! *Bad* Boog! No! No! No!" Then she opened the screen door and tossed him onto the porch with a *klump*!

The screen door bang-banged shut behind her.

Boog was disheveled and humiliated, and there was quite a bit of laughter coming from the tree in front of the house. Icarus was there with the other birds.

"*You!*" Boog ordered, pointing into the tree. "Get down here! *Now!*"

Icarus stopped laughing, as did the others, and glided to the porch railing.

"The kid has the cricket! Get me back that cricket!" Boog reached out and curled a long claw around Icarus's neck, then cinched it tight. "Or *else!*"

"...Okay. Sure thing, Boog. Soon as he comes out, I'll snatch him back. ...But then what?"

Boog's eyes widened, black and pitiless, then he snapped his jaws at Icarus and released him without a word. Icarus shot back into the tree. Boog slunk down the steps and crouched under the porch, impaling a hapless spider on a claw as he waited, then flicking it against the house with a quiet *plop!* without so much as a look to admire his murderous handiwork.

"Thank you," said Peter to Mrs. Barrow as he stepped out the door and onto the porch. The screen door bang-banged shut. Peter carefully lifted the Maestro from his front pocket and held him in his open hand as he came down the steps.

"I'm Peter Phye," he said. "And this is Dillon Hopper."

The Maestro looked from one to the other, then at Dillon. "A magicada," he said.

"That's right," said Dillon, sounding a bit surprised to be properly acknowledged.

"I've never had the pleasure before," the Maestro said. "To hear one for real, that is; only fey interpretations. I thought I was born in the wrong era to ever hear one. You're out of season... by many, many seasons."

Dillon blushed. "I was brought here from the Deep South," he said.

"The music of your kind is legendary," said the Maestro.

Peter placed the Maestro on his shoulder, alongside Dillon, as he walked around toward the back of Mrs. Barrow's house toward the meadow and the woods behind his own house.

"Please, Mr. Hopper, if you don't mind, will you play for me?" asked the Maestro.

Peter was eager himself to hear Dillon's music.

"Well," said Dillon, "I'm really not prepared..."

"Aw, go on Dillon," Peter interrupted. "I've been waiting a long time, too."

Dillon opened his vest, but before he was able to do any more, there was a *whoosh!* and the flap of wings, and the Maestro was gone!

A single blue feather twisted lithely to the ground.

"Whistler!" cried Dillon.

Icarus dove several times, hot-dogging in defiance, as Peter and Dillon chased after him, running and leaping into the air and shouting. Boog emerged from beneath the porch and watched. Icarus buzzed Peter's head, weaving recklessly through Mrs. Barrow's dangling unmentionables, then turned to jeer with a brazen *WAHH!*

"Stop playing around!" screamed Boog. "Bring him to me, *now!*"

Icarus circled back for another fly-by, when a curious wind began tossing the bloomers, bras, and stockings into a little dance on the lines. The wires jiggled and bounced, and Icarus Whistler, in all his arrogant bravado, caught himself on one of those wires, sending the Maestro and himself crashing to the grass on the lawn. Peter raced over and snatched the Maestro back into his pocket. The Maestro brushed at himself, then pulled Peter's pocket closed. Icarus, stunned and slightly injured, flopped around on the ground, trying to regain his senses, while Boog glided toward him, head low and body close to the ground.

"Chance!" Peter exclaimed. "You caused the breeze to blow!"

Chance winked from where he had appeared on Peter's shoulder beside Dillon.

"Nice work," Dillon said. Then added with a friendly smile, "For a quark."

"Any time," replied Chance, who smiled as they touched hands in a celebratory high-five.

"Just one more thing..." Chance said before disappearing again.

"Heel! ...*Heel!*" Pixie Anderson came loping across the yard behind Rex. Boog dashed back for cover under the porch. "I saw that, Phye! Good job, you almost killed 'em!"

Rex hurried ahead, barking and leaping up and down, nearly crushing the helpless, cowering bird. "Get away, you stupid, crappy dog!" Pixie caught up, and kicked Rex, who responded with a startled yelp. Then he grabbed Icarus. "Excellent! Now I have a bird, too!"

Pixie held Icarus to his face, nearly removing his scalp-feathers with rough caresses from his finger. Pixie was quite a sight himself, with dried, brown splotches of Calamine lotion dabbed onto the many bee stings about his pink legs and face and arms. "Come Rex!" he ordered, and hurried away. "Time for boot camp! *Yesss!* We have an air force! I'll be needing my surgical set-up. We'll have t' clip his wings till we get him trained."

"Don't feel too bad for him," said Dillon. "He got what he deserved."

"I can't help it," said Peter. "Even Icarus Whistler doesn't deserve a cruel a fate as Pixie."

"Feel bad for his parents," said Dillon. "They're really decent birds. Let's just call it Reform School. Icarus might eventually find his way back home. ...If he learns anything at all."

The sun glowed orange on the tips of the trees ahead of them. Peter waded through meadow grass toward the woods behind his house.

Chapter Thirty-nine
Ithaca

What a return to the woods it was! Every imaginable creature was there to greet them when Peter and Dillon finally found their way back. It began somewhere in the middle of the meadow, and continued the entire rest of the way.

"Good work, Peter!" and, "I knew you would do it!" they all said as he passed, patting him on the legs and flying onto his shoulders to kiss his cheeks. And, "Nice job! Well done!" and, "You did it, thank the Creator!" (This latter sort of remark from the broader minded, ecumenical birds).

Peter, of course, always loving animals as he did, was thrilled by the affection they showed him. The fairies flitted about, too, singing and cheering loudly in what reminded Peter of adults imitating children's voices. The Muse Laureate was there, smiling and hovering patiently above the polished stump. It seemed he was prepared to recite again. Peter was stunned by the reception, and by the fact that it was all for him and Dillon.

"How'd they know?" he asked.

"News travels fast in Efemera," said Dillon.

The Maestro peered out from Peter's pocket. The Commodore

was there, near the polished stump, with his arms extended and head cocked with a smile. Peter stopped and the crowd slowly fell quiet.

"Peter, my boy, you've done a tremendous thing."

"It was... fun," said Peter, and everyone cheered loudly.

The Maestro hopped onto Peter's shoulder and stood alongside Dillon. Peter saw him well for the first time. He was austere looking, with a shock of white on top, and a taut lower jaw that gave his face a distinct squareness. His face was indeed very striking.

"How are you, Commodore?" he asked.

"Very well," replied the Commodore. "Our baritone, however, and the frogs of the chorus have refused to be present. Seems they have a grievance to air and have been holding out." He raised a bushy eyebrow at Peter. "Unbeknownst to any of us until now."

"Well," said the Maestro, looking plainly at Dillon, "what would the Music Of The Night be without a baritone and Palladins?"

"Exactly," replied Dillon, nodding in sudden and total agreement. He met and looked quickly away from Peter's stunned and furtive glances.

The Maestro took Dillon's hand and thrust it over their heads, and the crowd broke immediately into frenzied cheering. The Maestro allowed it to continue for a few minutes, maintaining his pose and a dignified stoic expression. Dillon was less experienced in the gracious nuances of public adulation, and so looked decidedly uncomfortable beside the Maestro. The Maestro waved his arms to regain silence, then turned and bowed, arms open, toward Dillon. The hush became intense, and Peter felt nervous for Dillon, who looked around shyly, then leaned forward.

"I'm really not very good unaccompanied," he said to the Maestro, who simply shook his head and waved his hands at him as he stepped away.

"Nonsense," he said, then bowed again with a grandiose flourish.

Dillon reached into his vest and produced a simple, straight wood stick with a single string stretched along its length. It looked like he had whittled it himself and stuck a cardboard box to the end. In fact, the makeshift construction of this much anticipated and wondrous diddley-bow was actually a bit unsettling to Peter, who'd expected something a little more sophisticated if it was to be heard a mile away, like Dillon had bragged it would. A diddley-bow: the thing looked more like a flimsy little banjo than any wall-toppling, ear-splitting clarion, which is exactly what a kid like Peter imagined based on the scant clues provided. How else would anyone imagine a musical instrument they'd never heard or seen while being so heavily touted? Dillon looked up at him, and Peter just smiled and nodded.

And so, hesitantly at first, Dillon began to play.

He slid a tiny thimble under the string as he plucked it with his other hand, making a wonderfully melancholy sound, which Peter felt deep within his chest, startling in its brilliance. The Maestro closed his eyes and nodded as he listened, looking as if he were being carried away to some longed-for, far-off place. And after several minutes of this, he produced a fiddle of his own, one of shining, polished wood (and of obvious high quality) to join Dillon in a wondrous duet. From the first, it was clear the Maestro's mind worked in musical tones, and he poured them through his instrument as effortlessly as speaking. That was the extent of his mastery. So suited to one-another were he and his instrument that neither seemed separate from the other, or could ever be; which is to say, one would not know he was even holding an instrument unless they had known him without it... which would be impossible for anyone not expressly invited by the Queen to visit Efemera. The Maestro held his under his chin, a distinction, according to Dillon, along with the issue of quality, separating him from the grasshopper bumpkins, his distant relatives, who liked to hold theirs in the crook of a forearm and "saw off notes as fast as they were able." The Maestro was a grand improviser, dove-tailing and working effortlessly to compliment Dillon... who was no slouch either, his pitch sliding back and forth with a melodic, tremulous *twang*. The creatures of Efemera listened. Then, unable to contain themselves any longer, they joined in a grand improvisation of their own, bringing the woodland alive once more.

And so it was, and so it is: The Everything, meandering along with no apparent purpose, justified by its product of an occasional brilliant… *Now.*

Chance appeared in the air before Peter. "You've done an extraordinary thing, indeed," he said.

"Not really," said Peter, turning a bit red.

"Oh, but you have. You've set things right. And, in doing so, you've shown a high regard for the creatures of Efemera, such a rare thing for those among your kind."

"It was nothing," said Peter. "I'd do it all again."

"And I believe you," Chance said, smiling in a way that said he somehow knew for sure.

Dillon flew from Peter's shoulder. The Maestro leapt to follow.

"But you know the enchantment must end now," Chance said. "I'm afraid it's the nature of Efemera."

Peter lowered his eyes, feeling all at once what he had known since the adventure began. He was, after all and as he well knew, an outsider who'd found his way there precisely because things weren't right. He felt suddenly very sad and alone.

Chance understood.

"There is a place for all of us in The Forever someday, even for those who may not believe so. …Even for those incapable of believing so."

The Muse spoke:

> Earthbound. Still,
> I look to the skies.
> Spread my wings, away I go…
> I was, I am, will always be here,
> In a land of dreams,
> Keeper of ephemera,
> Weaver of the fabric, wispy thin…

And so, from amid the celebration, Chance led Peter out of Efemera, back between the oaks, mainly because, as the Queen had said, it could be unhealthy for a boy to tarry too long within wispy, fleeting moments. Life moves pretty fast, and young Peter, we should all be glad to know, while possessing all the natural gifts of a great philosopher, would later reflect upon his experiences in Efemera and conclude on his own that living in the moment is a good thing when done judiciously and in moderation. That way, a person always has something to look forward to, so to speak, because a person with nothing to look forward to will become an unhappy creature once they take notice of the fact.

Peter looked to his house. He was close now. His stomach gave a flutter. And it was there, from amid the morass of his own fear and loathing, that Peter began to realize the terrible price being paid by his mother to choose a life in exile from a moment they should rightly be sharing together. Life can bring you down, Peter had decided in his own abstract way, and one mustn't confuse it with living when they set out to discover its mysteries. Peter might become a man any minute now, while his mother was in limbo.

"You know," Chance said, "I turn choices into outcomes and guide the lines of confluence. Mine is the hand that weaves the tapestry of life." Chance flickered and nearly vanished. "And you are my friend."

Chance flickered again, and Peter thought he might have been lost.

"What about Lucien and the hobgoblin sleuths?" he asked quickly.

"Who?" replied the voice of Chance.

And then, there it was, as it was before, the lulling hiss of the wind through the leaves on the trees, but a part in the lilt of a song for a summer night.

Chapter Forty

Calypso

"**W**ho're you talkin' to?"

The voice startled Peter and he turned quickly. Francine Fenstermacher was there. Peter hadn't seen her since school had ended in June, and that seemed like forever ago now that he was looking at her again. She had been on vacation with her family and looked different than when he'd seen her last. Her eyes were different, and her smile, and the way she held her head... all different. Peter suddenly felt too embarrassed to talk to her, though he wished to, nonetheless.

"N-nobody," he stammered, turning to look again at the oaks. They seemed to nearly touch. The trees were grown together so that Peter knew he would never fit between them again. The pond was still there, though, and the music that played.

"Oh," said Francine. "Well, I just got home today. Whatcha been doin' all summer?"

She smiled in a way that made Peter's face warm.

"Ah... Ah... Nothin', really," he replied. "Playin' with bugs."

"I like bugs," Francine offered.

Wow, even more spectacular than he'd dreamed!

"I got a new CD player," Francine said. "Wanna listen t' CD's?"

"CD's?"

"Music."

Peter had never spent any time just listening to music before, but it suddenly seemed like a good idea.

Chapter Forty-one
Getting Rid Of A Bugaboo

It was dark when Peter arrived back home. Francine's mother and father had invited him to eat dinner with them, then all had walked with him to the edge of the meadow to the point just before they got to his house. Francine lived on the opposite shore of Peter's Sea of Queen Anne's Lace, in the house next to Pixie Anderson, down the road from Mrs. Barrow. Francine's parents told Peter they walked that way every night anyhow... a fact which Peter found hard to believe. They waited a long while before turning back home, until a light went on in Peter's house. Mrs. Fenstermacher looked at Mr. Fenstermacher with a worried expression.

Once home, Peter heard voices in the dark:

"Now, now, let's not be so hasty. A single bad outcome doesn't make the experience all bad."

"But I feel I'm losing control."

His mother and someone else were talking downstairs. A light was on in the basement, and Peter heard quiet music playing, the kind his mother had listened to in the days when she wasn't so angry all the time. Peter had entered quietly through the back door, careful not to let it slam. The darkened house told him his mother had been downstairs all day, or, at the very least, since sometime before dark. Peter stood at the stairway to listen:

"Don't you worry, milady, everything'll be just fine. Another drink, perhaps?"

Flynn? thought Peter. "Mom, is that you?" he asked.

Silence.

"Leave me alone, please," Mrs. Phye called up.

"Who're you talking to?"

Silence.

"Mom?"

"Nobody. Leave me alone."

"No need t' be so distant, milady. We all need friends. Let's have 'em down with us," said the voice of Flynn.

"Who's with you, mom?" Peter asked.

"Nobody."

"I recognize that voice," said Peter. "Who's there?"

"'Tis only me, Peter, beggin' yer pardon for scarin' you off the way I did."

"How do you know my son?" Peter heard his mother ask.

"Mom, I'm coming down," said Peter, afraid to disobey her, yet more afraid to leave her alone with the likes of Flynn.

"No!" she called up quickly.

"Ah, but I wouldn't say I know him yet, milady. Only just barely acquainted, we are. I found 'em wanderin' in the forest, all alone."

"You stay away from him, you hear me!"

"Yer takin' such a harsh tone, milady, and at me of all yer dearest companion. There's no need for gettin' excited."

"Mom, I know him! Is he your bugaboo?" Peter called down.

"My what? ...Yes. ...Ah, go on, Peter. Go to your room. I'll be up later."

"I *know* him! Get rid of him, mom! Throw him out!" Peter switched the kitchen light on and began to descend the steps.

"Out you go," he heard his mother say, emerging from around the corner at the bottom of the stairs, holding the fussing, cussing little Flynn between her fingers. (No need to mention the things he was yelling, which were quite foul.) He had a temper when things didn't go his way. Peter snatched the hat off his head as his mother passed. She held a whisky bottle in one hand and stuffed Flynn into it with the other, then corked it tight. Flynn stomped up and down in the bit of liquid that remained at the bottom and ranted in entombed silence with animated gesticulations through the glass. Mrs. Phye opened the back door and flung the bottle, end-for-end, into the trees, over the top of the wood pile.

Then she turned and hugged Peter, which she hadn't done in a very long time.

Chapter Forty-two
Rocco Colossimo Collects His Pay

Peter had left Efemera for a full day now, and the music played on. He looked into the woods and listened to the song as shadows turned the leaves a darker shade of green.

Gonk, Gonk, Gonk.

Peter smiled. It seemed the Maestro had found a way to satisfy Herr Placido, as Dillon said he would. Peter listened and thought it certainly worth the effort. However small his part might actually be in the scheme of an entire symphony, it was important.

He wondered how Dillon was getting on.

The season was waning, that was obvious now. School would start again soon. The subtle signs had been there all along, the browning of the leaves on certain trees and bushes; the fields, ready now to be picked; the general feeling that comes with the passing of July. Peter was suddenly immensely sad for the things he'd left behind, and not so much because he'd left them than that they had left him. From that time forward, he would know that beginnings implied endings, and that the time in between, whatever it really meant, was meant to be enjoyed.

"Ayeeeee!"

But his melancholy was broken by a scream! He ran to the house. Through the trees and past the wood pile. The screen door crashed open before he could reach it.

And Rocco Colossimo hurried out, puffing and wheezing, and lumbering ungainly and as fast as he was able, followed by his toady crew of calligraphers. Peter turned to watch as they passed and disappeared into the tangle of brush, now almost completely engulfed in shadow. Something shiny dangled from Rocco's mouth.

"Just look at what they did to my house!" his mother cried as she stood with her back to Peter in the doorway, the light from within showing the silhouette of a surprisingly attractive woman. She had been busy cleaning all day, and yet the house looked again as if it had been ransacked. Peter felt a sudden twinge of guilt.

"Hurry in and shut the door!" his mother said.

Peter stepped in. "Wow, mom, are you okay?" He looked around as the door banged itself closed behind him.

"Don't know," she said. "Check and see if there're any more. ...Those raccoons can have rabies, you know! Be careful. ...And those filthy little toads, hopping through my house!"

"They're gone, mom," Peter said. "I saw 'em run past me outside."

"There might be more," she said, as she flipped the hook to lock the screen door.

"Is anything missing?" Peter asked.

"I don't know. I'm too shook-up to know. It's all so messy again." His mother threw her hands atop her head. "And after all my hard work."

"It's not so bad, mom. I can help."

And so, Peter helped his mother to straighten up. The job soon calmed her. It was easy, being clean underneath, just a matter of up-righting and putting things back where they belonged. Rocco and his gang hadn't destroyed anything. That wasn't their way.

Purely business, that's all.

That night Peter lay in his bed and watched out the window as the music played. He was happy. Supper was good. His family had even had dessert together, chocolate tapioca pudding with whipped cream on top... and just enough of it, too! He'd laughed with his mom and dad as they talked about the things that had happened. Peter and his mom interrupted one another with explosive giggles and boisterous laughter as they took turns telling their versions of what had happened with the raccoon and toads.

A fresh sound began in the bush outside Peter's window. It was Dillon. Peter recognized him, and even Sisyphus, busy some-where across the meadow, stopped to listen and smile. Dillon's music was a marvel, reminding Peter of things vague and pleasant. He listened blissfully and thought he would long forever for the feelings the sounds evoked, and for the sounds that brought alive in him such feelings.

Peter drifted off to Dreamland.

Chapter Forty-three
Flynn's Final Appeal

"**P**sst! *Peter*! Over here!"

Peter set down the stick he was whittling and stood up on the steps of the back porch. He walked over to the wood pile, where he thought he'd heard someone call his name.

Flynn was there, hiding behind the stack of logs.

"What's that on your head," Peter asked, because Flynn looked ridiculous. Rather than being bald, Flynn wore a perfectly coiffured head of black hair, styled in a dashing, wavy pompadour (very much, Peter noted, like that of Major John Grande, the astronaut gone AWOL from his toy collection). Flynn frowned as he rolled his eyes upward and reached to adjust the absurd thing.

"And how'd you get outta the bottle?" added Peter, suddenly less concerned about bad hairpieces.

"Aw, it took some doin', that's for sure," said Flynn. "The big fella found me idle on the Sea of Rye. Unstopped the bottle and I danced round his tongue till he found the liquid more distractin'. And (he said this next part with a touching show of humility) oh, I'm so grateful t' say! I'm here now t' tell ya 'bout it."

"What big fella?"

"The 'coon and his toadies. They went hoppin' toward your house when they were done."

"Rocco Colossimo?"

"Aye, that's him," said Flynn. "Raccoon and dealer of contraband crap!" he muttered unhappily, fiddling to readjust his canted hairline.

Peter began walking back toward the house.

"Wait!" called Flynn. "T'was days ago. You saw him comin' out that night."

Peter stopped and looked back. "You know what he took?"

"Maybe," said Flynn with a sly grin.

"Never mind," said Peter, turning again to leave.

"Oh, Peter?" said Flynn. Peter stopped and looked back. "Peter, I'm afraid I'm not quite the same laddie without m'hat. It's not safe out here without one. I've been feelin' naked and vulnerable. I've seen Oblivion, and I'm afraid I may end m'days passin' through the gut of some rodent. I've seen the light." Flynn smiled hopefully, "Could you..." He clapped his hands together and held them out. "Please?"

"Too late," Peter said, and pointed to the toadstools growing on the ground alongside the wood pile. "You'll have to live on your own from now on, and not off others. Maybe your friends will help you."

"*Friends!* What friends?" Flynn turned ugly. "They ignore me now and pretend I don't exist! I'll get me hat back, I will, and you'll be hearin' from me again, that you can count on!"

"Shush, you! I'd banish you to Oblivion right now if I were a cruel person!" snarled Peter. "But I expect you'll find your own way there unless you change your ways. ...And I hope you do. Until then, you just do what I say and stay far away from my house!" Peter smiled and looked at the toadstools. "And I'll just tend to my garden."

Flynn snatched a twig from the wood pile and snapped it angrily in his hands, then ran over and tugged like a madman on one of the toadstools -- which didn't budge -- his spindly little arms tightening and slackening like two rubber bands as his body heaved. And in all the heaving and hoing, his wig slipped forward over his eyes. He snatched it off in a snit and drop-kicked it toward the weeds, where it hung up high in the murderous barbs of the pickers, looking to Peter likely harder than the old soup can to retrieve. Flynn stopped and stared at it himself, running a hand slowly forward and back again over his head; and then the thought of the difficulty involved in fetching it back likely dawned on him, and he dropped and flailed about on the ground in one filthy little tirade.

Peter didn't stay for it... entertaining as it was and still promised to be. He just shook his head, then turned and walked away.

Chapter Forty-four
Coda

The leaves were colored. The day was warm. Indian summer. Peter wore a blue T-shirt. He thought again of the heat of August, and it made him think of how autumn always finds one so quietly. Like sleep.

He thought of Dillon and would always think of Dillon on days such as these. He hadn't seen him since he left him in Efemera, since he left him in those waning days of summer. He had hoped to find him again though, especially this day, and was therefore understandably excited to see him on the back porch that morning.

"Oh! Dillon!" Peter leaned over and picked him up.

Peter's father was with him.

"Ah, a katydid," he said.

"A magicada," said Peter.

"Very good," his father said. "I thought I'd been hearing one, but then I thought I must be imagining things. They're not due for another ten years at least."

"Isn't he a handsome example of his kind?" Peter said, admiring him as he held him out.

"It's good luck to find one out of season, you know," Peter's father said. Then he smiled wistfully. "Afraid it's the end, though. I'm surprised he survived last week's frost. Not likely to survive many more."

There was the sadness. Peter tried to keep it behind him. He and Dillon had long since lost the ability to talk to one another.

*　　　*　　　*

Peter looked out the small window of the airplane as it soared between thick, puffy clouds. The sight was breathtaking. Way up here amid the clouds was a whole other world, filled with waterfalls and misty mountaintops, and the vastness of everything above. And Peter was part of it. He breathed in deep and imagined he could stand atop the clouds and leave the cares of the world beneath him. And when his father was asleep, he reached into his pocket. He held Dillon on the palm of his hand at the window, and they gazed out, knowing all the while that each was echoing the other's thoughts, precisely.

*　　　*　　　*

At the edge of the woods, near the back of Peter's uncle's yard, was a river and the most fascinating trees Peter had ever seen. Their roots grew down from the branches and were twisted into odd shapes and sizes, making each a unique work of art. And from somewhere amid their boughs came a most exquisite and distinctive buzzing. Peter had never before been so vividly reminded of happy times. They were Dillon's kind, making musical strains, flowing in waves from one tree to another.

He reached again carefully into his pocket and held Dillon out on the back of his hand.

"The secret Chance told me that day was this," he said. "We all live in a Realm of Possibility."

They looked at one another and all was understood.

"I'll never forget you," Peter said.

Dillon chirped, then flew away into the banyan trees, their beauty now all the more splendid.

The End

About The Author

Mark Dennis is a dentist, writing from White Lake, Michigan, where he has a son, Nicholas - grown up now and off to college - and a wife, Camille. *Song For a Summer Night* is a book about the idylls of his boyhood, and the unsustainable, lazy days of summer, so carelessly spent.

**This Book Is Also Available
In A Kindle Edition**